Abo

Dr. Keith Fisher has been a chemist all his working life. He was born in Birmingham in 1940 during the bombing. Passing the 11 plus allowed him to go to a grammar school in Smethwick.

Leaving school, he worked in chemical laboratories and did his degree part-time. After graduation he went to Canada to start a post-graduate degree which he finished at the University of London with a Ph.D.

Post-doctoral studies and several teaching positions at universities in America took up the next five years. Returning to the UK he took up a senior lectureship at the University of Lagos followed by a post at the

University of Khartoum. After nearly thirteen years in Africa, he spent two years in Canada before coming to Australia in 1989.

His Uncle Percy was a great story teller and that stirred his interest in short stories.

EXPATS IN NIGERIA

Keith Fisher

EXPATS IN NIGERIA

Vanguard Press

VANGUARD PAPERBACK

© Copyright 2021
Keith Fisher

The right of Keith Fisherr to be identified as author of
this work has been asserted by him in accordance with the
Copyright, Designs and Patents Act 1988.

All Rights Reserved

No reproduction, copy or transmission of this publication
may be made without written permission.
No paragraph of this publication may be reproduced,
copied or transmitted save with the written permission of the
publisher, or in accordance with the provisions
of the Copyright Act 1956 (as amended).

Any person who commits any unauthorised act in relation to
this publication may be liable to criminal
prosecution and civil claims for damages.

A CIP catalogue record for this title is
available from the British Library.

ISBN 978-1-80016-129-0

*Vanguard Press is an imprint of
Pegasus Elliot MacKenzie Publishers Ltd.*
www.pegasuspublishers.com

First Published in 2021

**Vanguard Press
Sheraton House Castle Park
Cambridge England**

Printed & Bound in Great Britain

Dedication

To my first wife, Janet, and my three children,
Teresa, Alex and Sarah.

Acknowledgements

I wish to thank two old school friends, Dave Lawrence and Tony Homer, for reading some of the stories and giving helpful advice. I also wish to thank Midge Dean, the wife of one of my colleagues, for lots of welcome advice.

Nigeria
Ikeja Club

Ikeja was on the outskirts of Lagos (It's now just part of the sprawl called Lagos.) quite close to the airport. Lagos was the fastest growing city in Africa and far outstripping its infrastructure. The expatriate community, which was not insubstantial, was separated into three or four enclaves, Victoria Island, Lagos Island, Apapa and the area around the airport including Ikeja. Life in Nigeria for the expatriate was very dependent on location, facilities provided by the company and how well the person could adapt to the heat, humidity and the people. The expatriate community in Ikeja was a very mixed bunch, English, Irish, French, German, Italian, Egyptians, Lebanese, Syrians, Iraqi and South Africans. There were one or two Americans but they were mostly concentrated in Lagos and Victoria Island.

Before 1960, i.e., before independence, this area had been sparsely populated with foreigners although the airport had attracted some Nigerians and a few expatriates. Where expatriates gathered there was the need for a meeting place — a club. Land and a substantial building were acquired from the government at a peppercorn rent — one pound per year. The Lagos

Country Club was formed, colloquially known as the Ikeja Club.

The land was not big enough for a golf course but there was space for a substantial building with a swimming pool, tennis courts and squash courts. The main hall was configured so that badminton and dancing could take place. There was also a theatre, as well as a snooker room and bars. Initially the members were expatriates with some wealthy Nigerians. On the adjoining piece of land, a school was built for the children under ten of expatriate and Nigerian members.

In the early years the club had a strict dress code but that had to be relaxed due to the heat and humidity in Lagos. However, some older "colonials" still dressed formally, for the men with a jacket and tie and for the ladies with a dress; no shorts or slacks. Not all of the rooms could be air conditioned but a lounge called the Ward room (after one of the Presidents) was more formal and although a jacket might not be required, a collar, tie, long trousers and shoes were expected. Of course Nigerian dress with a full flowing (Agbada) gown was okay. The ladies also had to be dressed conservatively (that was a hard one to judge but shorts were out). The club was run by a committee of members.

We came to Lagos in 1974 and were soon members of the Lagos Country Club. Although the fees seemed a bit steep there was no other place in the vicinity where we could really relax and take our children to play in safety. In Nigeria it was important to relax outside the home; on the street or in the traffic it was a tense place. Every day you could see something new and it was not always pleasant — I termed it an adrenaline place, as you always had to be on your guard. Out in Lagos, because of my colour I was assumed to be rich. There were a lot of rich expatriates but I was not one of them. Yes, I was rich compared with the average Nigerian I could meet on the street but there were many Nigerians much richer than me.

The club was a meeting place and although many of the expatriate members would only be in Lagos for a short time it was also a place to make friends. The mix of nationalities made it a very interesting place to meet people. The women possibly made more friends than the men as they often spent more time in the club. Being outside one's homeland may free up some attitudes and talk, that being at home one would be more discreet about. As an example, there were always Irish people around, some from Northern Ireland and some from Eire, Catholics and Protestants. On occasions there were sing-songs, they could all sing the Republican songs and the Sash, a Protestant song. Also, Arabs, not necessarily friends at home, had a common language and could "tolerate" each other.

We learnt lots of things from our new friends. Our Iraqi friend told us about her dowry which she would get back if she ever left her husband or vice versa. Of course he would never leave her nor she him, and the dowry of 250 pounds was not going to last long. Mixed-marriage friends had lots of different stories about their arrival and life in Nigeria.

The hall was used for many events and large gatherings were common. Members loved to dance but the only bands available for dances were local Nigerian (Yoruba) bands and then the mixing really got enjoyable. Europeans tend to dance more vigorously than the locals, in the heat and humidity this meant you became very sweaty and exhausted in a short time. The Nigerians, particularly the women, would move much slower to the music and many expats learned to dance in their style.

Besides the social activities there were sporting activities that brought people together. Cricket, tennis and football were weekend sports played by many members. Our cricket team played in a league with many Nigerian teams and our record against them was poor. The West African Cricket Association could never seem to get their act together as two forces, Nigeria and Ghana, always seemed at odds. There were several good young Nigerian players who equipped themselves well when a touring English club came to play. We attempted to get a scholarship for one young player to spend time in the UK, but to no avail. Football was the most frequently played sport, and one funny incident comes to mind: I was driving with a Nigerian friend when we stopped for a Catholic procession lead by an Irish priest I knew. As they passed my Nigerian friend recognised the priest and said he had played football against him and that he was the dirtiest player on the field, with the foulest mouth. All I could say was that he probably enjoyed some free time.

After our first year of membership, I was roped in to become the secretary — I think I was elected unopposed as no one else wanted the job. With a diverse membership there were a diverse number of complaints, most were verbal but some were in writing. Most of the complaints were about the behaviour when a member had drunk too much. There were very few complaints about the staff and we had a manager who could handle such complaints. Our monthly committee meetings were generally taken up with complaints about members. Some of the meetings could go on for hours. The other problem was finances, with the American treasurer at odds with the Nigerian entertainments' secretary. As with all clubs we had to be careful of money being 'siphoned' off by members or staff. The chairman, an elderly Nigerian, we called Doc was not very adept at handling these situations and committee meetings.

After a couple of years some of my friends said I should stand against the Doc, as by that time I was well known about the club. I had acted in two plays put on in the club theatre and many of the Nigerian members were very pleased with our productions, as there was little live theatre in Lagos. My election was not universally received, however, as some Nigerian

15

members thought it a retrograde step. I tried to keep committee meetings as short as possible but the nature of the committee meant that there was always some conflict. I also tried to make sure the finances were going in the right direction and we were able to sort out a few 'rorts'. After a couple of years, I decided that my enjoyment of the club was being diminished by being chairman and I stood down. The following chairman was a Nigerian and by that time the Nigerian members outnumbered the expatriates.

I recently talked to an expatriate who lived near Ikeja and asked about the Ikeja Club. He didn't know the club but there was a Nigerian club he had never visited. The club is still in existence and by the look of their internet pages doing very well.

The expatriate has many problems but isolation from the surrounding community can be one of the biggest. The club served a good purpose for my family and I.

Bar Beach Lagos

"Let's go to the beach it's boring at the club with no swimming pool," my youngest daughter kept repeating insistently. She must have learned repetition from me, if you said it often enough it might be heard and acted upon. Actually, all three of my children had kept up a barrage of requests and suggestions we go to the beach, ever since they had learnt that the club pool would be closed on Saturday. "Our friends are going to Bar Beach and the club will be deserted."

We did go to Bar Beach, about once a month, but generally on a Sunday when the roads were less full of traffic. This time they wanted to go on a Saturday; I was dreading the traffic jams. I was playing cricket on Sunday so they knew this was their only chance to go to the beach.

Bar Beach was on Victoria Island and we lived in Ikeja which would mean a drive through the centre of Lagos on a shopping day. I was reluctant to say yes as the crowds and traffic jams on a Saturday morning would be horrendous. But I finally gave in and my three children were ecstatic. Their mother was happier than I so I thought I must make the best of the situation. Thinking it over, I had come to the conclusion that if I picked the time correctly then the traffic might not be too bad. On Saturdays, cars having licence plates with an even first number were allowed on to the main road into Lagos (in the week they were allowed on Tuesdays and Thursdays). The main road to Lagos was called the Ikorodu Road, it had an unenviable reputation for accidents.

At nine thirty in the morning, we set off and as we passed the Country Club there was a spontaneous cheer from the back seat. My wife smiled and I chuckled to myself. Living in Lagos was not too difficult for the kids and going to the beach once a month would have been heaven for me at their age. Living in Birmingham as a child there had been no beach within more than a hundred miles.

I thought that if we were lucky, we might be at the beach by 11 a.m. but if we were unlucky who knows what time we would get there. The beach was only fifteen miles away but even on a quiet Sunday, it took us an hour.

Our route took us from Ikeja to Maryland where we entered the infamous Ikorodu Road. This road had a nasty reputation for accidents — especially at night, but at least we were doing it in daylight. We would take the road through various named places to Iddo where there was a large market near the Railway Terminal. After Iddo we would cross the Carter Bridge into Lagos Island and then would have two choices. Possibly the shortest way was through the centre of Lagos but the better route and often the quicker, though longer, was the Marina. I chose the Marina as there were possibly less hold-ups and the scenery was better. From the Marina we would cross the bridge onto Victoria Island and drive to the end of the road to Victoria Beach, commonly called Bar Beach. I had rehearsed all this in my mind and I was praying there would be no road blocks, due to accidents or demonstrations.

We were making good time when we reached the Ikorodu Road, the traffic was light. We were following a Land Rover and I was contemplating overtaking him when he suddenly pulled out into the next lane. I followed suit assuming there was a broken-down vehicle in the inside lane. My wife saw the reason first and quickly looked back at the children who were luckily chatting as we passed a well-hit corpse. I saw it but I couldn't identify male or female, even with a longer look I'm not sure whether I could identify the sex anyway. It was not uncommon to see a body on the side of the road but there would generally be boxes or stones around the body to make the traffic divert, but this body had not been afforded that courtesy. My wife looked very pale as I think this was the first dead body she had seen, I kept silent so that the children were not alerted.

We were approaching a place called Yaba, this was the district of the University of Lagos, when the traffic slowed and then came to a stop. So much for my plan, we were only about half way and the 'go slow' had started. I told my wife it was probably an accident and hopefully when we passed it the traffic would thin out and we would make better time. Six little ears had heard me and they were all looking around for an interesting sight, I had unfortunately aroused their curiosity. We slowly moved forward and approached a policeman who was directing the two-lane traffic into one lane. I then noticed lots more policemen and I thought this must be a major accident. My son saw it first and casually said to his sisters, "Did you see that hand?" I then saw it through the corner of my eye and I snapped, "Sit down and shut up, no one is to look on this side, look on the other side of the road." I was sweating and feeling a bit sick, my wife had covered her eyes with her hands and I was not sure whether my instructions were being followed. What my son had seen were pieces of a human body or bodies. These bodies had not been involved in a road accident, and I later learned what had happened to them. Robbers had broken into the house of a widow and she had raised the alarm and her neighbours had caught the robbers, lynched and then dismembered them. The body parts had been scattered on the road as a warning to other would-be robbers. This story was told to me the following Monday at work by a colleague who told it as though it was an everyday occurrence. He also showed me a newspaper article to back up his story.

I was feeling terrible and as the traffic started to move faster, I stuck my head out of the window to get a breeze on my sweaty face. The children were quiet in the back seat and my wife had a blank look. I had become hardened to some strange sights but the body at Maryland and the body parts had taken me by surprise. Finally, my wife told me not to stop at the market and I agreed. We had planned to buy some fruit for the beach. As we approached the market the traffic slowed to a crawl and we were able to buy some fruit from young boys, plying their wares down the traffic lanes. This was quite common in Lagos and in traffic jams you could buy girly magazines, cigarettes and decorations for your car, these were the most common items but as we were near the market it was fruit and vegetables. The back seat had been quiet since my outburst but the oranges and bananas had changed that and they were soon chatting about the ships lined up to go into the harbour. I was waiting for the mention of human parts and was glad that they had either forgotten or were avoiding Dad's wrath. This part of the drive was pleasant, but the speed was reduced by people dodging the traffic to cross the road, there were no organised crossing points and I'm sure there were several fatalities on this road. As we crossed onto Victoria Island you could hear the waves coming in from the Bight of Benin, it was very pleasant as the temperature seemed to drop a few degrees. The colour in my wife's cheeks had come back and she was smiling.

Driving along the road to the beach we noticed how few cars there were. On a Sunday the beach road would usually be full of cars with many parked on the median strip. Most of the expatriates drove to the end of the road to an area of the beach called Liverpool, I never found out why it was called that — why Liverpool? As I drove along, I could see a few free spaces near the end of the road but a casual look at the beach revealed it was almost deserted. One young Nigerian beckoned us into a space he was "guarding" but I passed him as I wanted to go as near to the end of the road as possible. Nearing the end, I saw a boy called John who had minded our car before so I pulled into "his space". Car-minding was probably necessary as the youths in this area seemed to like hub caps and possibly other removable car parts.

We pulled into John's spot and started to remove all our gear and cold box from the boot. I was approached by the boy I had just ignored.

"I'll look after your car," he said very loudly close to my ear.

"No, John will do that."

"I saw you first."

"No. I said John will look after my car," I said in a loud aggressive tone.

I was feeling irritated when he had not taken no for an answer and he would not shut up. He was talking very fast and loud in a mixture of Pidgin English and Yoruba. I caught a couple of curses and Oibo (white man or man with peeled skin) and realised I was not his favourite person. John stood by with a grin but didn't intercede. I was ignoring this loud youth and said to John, "Please mind my car I'll see you later."

This upset the youth and he started into a tirade much of which I didn't understand but he was annoying me. I turned to my wife and said "I hear someone talking but I see no one."

She replied, "Neither do I."

The youth jumped in front of me and shouted, "I'm here." As I was taller than him, I looked over the top of his head and said, "I see no one." I was now starting to enjoy the fun and I motioned to my wife to take the children to the beach. She was not enjoying the fun, so I said, "I'll join you when I have checked that everything on the car is locked."

Off she set with the anxious children and I slowly and methodically checked all the doors and the boot. The youth followed me and was telling me his family owned this land, his father was a chief and his brother a general and I should treat him well. I turned, looked at him and said, "I see no one, you are nothing." I was laughing inside but realised I should get out of this situation as a crowd was gathering.

The youth's reply was predictable. If you have ever heard a Nigerian argument (the first person says something and the next person repeats the statement and that can go on for a while). The youth's eyes seemed to be bulging as he said, "You are nothing." "I'm written about in books and my name will live when I die" I said with a big smile on my face. That took him aback and I took the opportunity to head for the beach. I half expected him to follow me but as I looked back, I could see him haranguing the laughing crowd. John was sitting on my car laughing at the youth who was gesticulating at the crowd.

I soon caught up with my wife and children who were labouring through the thick sand. The beach was so different from a Sunday; there was no organisation. Normally we would have been met by young children offering us deck chairs, palm-frond shelters, cold drinks (even a cold beer) or fruit. There were always traders with smuggled liquor. You had to be careful as a friend bought a bottle of Johnny Walker Black Label to find out later it was tea. Today the shelters were there but no other amenities. There were very few expats and the kids couldn't see any of their friends. Another problem was that the sea was very rough and although my children were better swimmers than their parents, they would be no match for the crashing surf. My wife was obviously worried about the danger and suggested we sit near a family with young children. Finally, we settled next to a couple with a young son, at least four adults would be a match for two girls and two boys.

I told my children not to dare to go near the sea without an adult accompanying them. They heeded my warning for a short time but after a while I had to go to the water's edge to order them back up the beach. The adults were having a miserable time trying to keep tabs on all the children and it was getting hotter and hotter. We had little time to relax until we persuaded them to make sand castles.

The couple we were next to were Egyptians and they were happy their son had other children to play with on the sand. They were both from the Egyptian Embassy and were having a miserable time in Nigeria. All their acquaintances outside the embassy were rich merchants who were always throwing lavish parties. In the embassy there was a strict hierarchy and different "stations" didn't mix. They were from Aswan which made them sort of "outcasts" and they were often referred to as Sudanese. I had noticed they were much darker than the other Egyptians we had met, in the airport hotel when we arrived in Sudan. We had met some Egyptian pilots attached to the Nigerian Air Force and they were very light-skinned. Similarly, our Iraqi, Lebanese and Syrian friends were very light-skinned. Our Syrian friend said these black people were not really Arabs but were better than the Egyptians. The Egyptians always seemed to be the butt of Arab jokes and even the Egyptians told Egyptian jokes as the English tell Irish jokes and the Irish make fun of themselves.

Our afternoon was really spoilt when they told of the death of five of their countrymen. Five of them, attached to the Nigerian Air Force had gone to a night club in Lagos and were heading for the airport late at night. Their car was speeding along the fast lane of the Ikorodu Road when they hit a broken-down truck. The truck had no lights and they ploughed into it so hard that the back axle of the truck was pushed forward several feet. Four had died before they could be rescued from the wreck and the fifth was flown to Cairo but died in a hospital. Our new-found friends seemed to be happy he died in Cairo but all we could think of was fitting names to faces.

We had spent a couple of weeks in the airport hotel in Ikeja when we first arrived in Sudan. There were four or five Egyptians attached to the Nigerian Air Force who seemed to be permanent residents of the hotel. We used to play cards with them and they enjoyed seeing our kids. I have two abiding memories of our hotel stay; one was a small black mamba being cornered by the staff in a walkway from the main hotel building to the rooms. We had ushered the children past the problem but they couldn't take their eyes off the snake and kept asking what would happen to the snake. The second less distinct memory was of very frequent use of the toilets; even our Egyptian friends had "tummy troubles" but maybe the children either suffered in silence or didn't let us know.

My wife and I were both thinking of our drive home and the sad events we had heard; I wanted to make sure we got home before dark. I made the excuse to the Egyptians that it was too hot for us. We called the kids and after many protestations about the time we said goodbye to our new friends. As we approached the car, I had a good look to see that there were four wheels and an intact windscreen. John was sitting on the car. It then occurred to me that this was the first time we had been to the beach and not been asked to buy smuggled liquor. I had bought whisky before and before payment had tried it to make sure it was not tea. Today the smugglers and trinket sellers had been absent.

I paid John, we all piled into the car and it started first time, so we set off towards home. We had not gone far when we were stopped by a policeman and there was a police car blocking the road — we had not yet reached the end of the beach. My initial smile was gone and I was wondering what could have happened on this quiet road. The policeman motioned that I should cross the median strip and drive on the wrong side of the road. As I drove along, I could see the problem, there was a lorry and they were unloading large tree trunks and planting them in the sand about fifteen feet apart. I watched for a time before I realised what was happening. They were planting stakes for tomorrow's executions. My wife also realised, she said "armed robbers". A voice came from the back, "What are they doing, Dad?"

"They are trying to grow trees on the beach."

That seemed to satisfy my young daughter and we soon passed the "planting".

As we accelerated along the beach road and passed the Federal Palace Hotel I turned to my wife and said, "I'm not coming here on a Saturday, too many people die."

Old Johnny

Johnny had been in Nigeria for thirty years or maybe twenty-five years or as little as twenty years, it was hard to tell. I had heard him tell the story several times but it was different each time. Some points in the story didn't vary: he had been in the British Army during World War II and his first encounter with Africa was in Egypt. He had later come to Nigeria but exactly when was never clear. The finer points of every story varied with Johnny's alcoholic consumption. The story he told me after the consumption of one Gulder beer was different from the story he told me later in the evening after several Gulder beers. The stories became more fanciful as the evening wore on. Once, he told me he had deserted in Egypt and stole a truck. Another time he had deserted in Italy and stole a truck and a third time a whole regiment had deserted in Italy. It seemed to me that there might be some truth in his desertion but he was not sure of the long-ago events and made the stories up to please the listeners.

I first saw Johnny in a hotel in Yaba, near the University of Lagos. My wife and I had been taken out by our new Nigerian friends to see some of the sights of Lagos. The place was a notorious hangout for prostitutes (we found that out later). I summed up the situation and was glad to be with my wife. There was a cabaret and lots of dancing and then there was Johnny, the only other white man in the room. He was dancing with the most beautiful Nigerian woman I had seen. By this time my friends had pointed out that there were a few prostitutes around and I assumed she was one of them. My eyes were focussed on Johnny; he was a small slim man dressed in shorts and a short-sleeved shirt. What was funny to me was that he was wearing sandals with socks. He looked to be about sixty but was dancing like a much younger man. His skin was very white and his legs had knotted veins, his hair was thin and mainly white with traces of ginger. What was most appealing about him was his smile, which was inexplicably infectious. During the dance he noticed me and nodded but we didn't speak on that occasion.

We had joined the Ikeja Country Club and it was several months before I saw Johnny again. The first thing I noticed was that he was with the same woman. They were sitting at the bar and she seemed to be trying to get him to leave. I thought nothing of it and went to join my wife and our friends in the lounge. After a while I heard a lot of shouting coming from the bar and our friends informed us that Johnny's wife was trying to get him home before he got hammered. They told us some of Johnny's story, most of which was confirmed by Johnny — only the way he told it was anti-Johnny.

Johnny called himself a steel erector: very few expats in Nigeria would have called themselves by such a lowly title; most were Managing Directors or General Managers or some other elevated title. Johnny owned his own company in his wife's name and I assumed he chose a title that was a slap in the face to the other expats.

Ivy, his wife, an Ibo girl, had been married to a soldier who had fought for Biafra in the civil war. Her husband had been killed and left Ivy and her baby to fend for themselves. They had little chance of survival in eastern Nigeria, so she set out for Lagos. Johnny had picked her up on the road and brought her to Lagos. They were definitely married as one or two of his old friends had attended the ceremony. Ivy was the most beautiful lady in the club, white or black. She had refused every proposal put to her and I witnessed one myself. A German was aggressively propositioning her but she politely but firmly put his ardour to rest. I talked to Ivy a few times and her English was very good. I learned she had gone to a Catholic school in the area that was then known as Biafra.

I got to know Johnny over a couple of years and I found our political views were quite similar but different from most of our expatriate colleagues. Johnny when sober was not the fool everyone thought. As a young man he had been a socialist and Bevan was his hero. He had once attended an Oswald Moseley rally (brown shirts) and had almost been swayed by Moseley's oratory. Later, on reflection, he realised the problems with Mosley's rhetoric. When the war ended, he had been demobbed and then disillusioned when Churchill was later returned to power so he left England. According to Johnny, Churchill had made a mess of Ireland, had been great during the war, but after the war stood for everything Johnny was against. He called it a 'class and moneyed society' and he wanted no part of it. I think he had tried to talk politics with other Brits and was surprised when I shared many of his views. Most Brits I had met were so conservative they would have been friends with Cecil Rhodes.

I asked Johnny why he had come to Nigeria and not Kenya or South Africa. Johnny's answer was simple; he had joined the merchant navy and enlisted on a 'tramp' cargo ship. They had set sail from Liverpool bound for the West African coast. Johnny hated the ship and the sea, and at the first stop, Accra, he had decided to jump ship but the opportunity didn't arise. At the second stop, Lagos, he went ashore and got lost. At that stage Nigeria didn't look like a land of opportunity but he was able to get a job in the construction industry. He had worked for Brits, Lebanese, Syrians and Italians (never for Germans). They had fixed up his visas and he quickly learnt a new trade. These were learning years and he made many friends of various nationalities. Johnny was a quick learner and he saw plenty of opportunities in the market. He now had a company in his wife's name, and jobs so plentiful he had a workforce of over fifty.

Whenever he mentioned his wife, I noticed a quiver in his voice — he was really proud of Ivy and his step daughter. During our talks once Ivy was mentioned there was a passion lacking in other parts of the story. Politics, Ivy and his daughter seemed to bring out much more emotion than other subjects. He didn't hide his feelings and that trait endeared me to him.

I talked to Ivy and found she was not only beautiful but also very intelligent. She informed me that the Ibos were the most educated Nigerians due to their being brought up as Christians. She quite openly talked about the Biafra war and how she met Johnny. He had been on his way back from a construction site and she was sitting on the side of the road feeding her daughter. Johnny stopped and offered her a lift, she had expected he would need a reward but Johnny had taken her to Lagos put her up in his flat and asked for nothing. Johnny had definitely prevented her from becoming a prostitute by providing her with shelter and food for her daughter. She knew many of the "night eagles" (many of them were Ibo girls) and was very glad she had not been forced to share their life-style. Lagos was an ugly place for a good-looking Ibo girl escaping eastern Nigeria. She knew Johnny's problems; he drank too much when he was not occupied with work. When sober she could manage him but it was more difficult when he was drunk. She knew that many members of the club both white and Nigerian regarded him as a drunken, crude fool. Ivy defended Johnny as best she could, but often she would have to revert to something like, "That's Johnny's way." She admitted he was worse when he returned from a job outside Lagos. On the job Johnny worked hard and drank little — he was building warehouses all over the country and was always there when they erected the steel framework. It was when he arrived in Lagos and found a bar or club and plenty of beer, then the problems started. Sometimes he would come straight home with gifts for Ivy and her daughter, then he would shower and change. She knew he was always going to the club. Other times she didn't have a clue where he would be drinking. She had a chance to drag him home if he went to the club, otherwise he could be gone for a couple of days. She was in charge of the company and could phone the building sites and knew when he should be in Lagos but could do nothing until he returned.

My problem with Johnny started when I became secretary of the club. I was continually getting complaints about his foul language and rude behaviour. These complaints were not only from women but also from men. I tried to point out that Johnny's swear words were old fashioned and not deserving the kinds of punishment suggested. For a while the complaints stopped and I assumed Johnny was out of town. Knowing what Ivy had told me I dreaded his return; my only hope was that he would go to a hotel rather than the club. Johnny didn't do as I had hoped and his return was a bad one. Johnny had returned from Ibadan, gone home and changed and then had come to the bar, continuously drinking for four hours. The barman later recounted that Johnny had gone to sleep on one of the bench seats in the bar, and that when he was awoken he was fighting mad.

I walked into the club at about 8 p.m. and heard shouting coming from the bar. The guards had pre-warned me that there was a problem and Johnny's name was mentioned. I almost went back to my car to drive home, but I entered the bar to find Johnny prancing around like a Victorian prize fighter. He had his fists raised in an old-style boxing pose and was challenging anyone to fight him. My initial reaction was that it was not too serious until I noticed a Nigerian member being physically restrained by a couple of his friends. I approached Johnny and asked him to come outside for a chat. His abuse was pretty strong and initially I was angry but decided the best thing to do was laugh. My laughter was abruptly stopped by a beer bottle breaking at my feet; now I had a problem. Johnny had just picked up a second bottle when into the bar walked Ivy; she walked past me and grabbed Johnny's arm. There was silence as she said "Let's go," and I watched in disbelief as they strolled past me out of the bar and out of the club.

Everyone was dumbfounded and it seemed to take a long time before the hush that had descended on the bar was broken. The lull should have been my cue to leave the bar but I needed a beer after that altercation. I was then inundated with everyone's opinion; disgusting behaviour, lunatic, senile filthy man with a filthy tongue, ban him, throw him out of the club; you name it, they said it. I thought that by letting everyone have their say it would all cool down, but I was wrong. My next tactic was to ask one person to tell the whole story. They all volunteered so I picked an older member of the club thinking that he might be more sympathetic to Johnny. Even I couldn't forget the broken bottle at my feet, but I was swayed by Ivy's handling of the situation.

The member showed none of my forgiving tendencies and he laid it on good and thick. The words came loud and fast and there was not a good word for Johnny. He had been drinking all afternoon and had fallen asleep on one of the bench seats in the bar. A group of Nigerians had come into the bar and found only a few seats vacant, one of them had woken Johnny. He had ill- advisedly told Johnny if he wanted to sleep, he should go home. Johnny's stream of Yoruba curses had been eloquent enough to take the Nigerian by surprise, but then an expat had tried to intervene. That set off the chain of events that had been in progress when I arrived. One of the Nigerians then started to explain the meaning of the curses that had rained down on them. I decided that any member who had a complaint should write a letter to the committee. I was swiftly out manoeuvred as one member had quickly written a complaint and ten signatures were attached as I watched. A napkin was presented to me with the firm instruction that the full committee should read and deliberate on the complaint. I decided to talk to Johnny before the committee meeting. The day before the meeting I caught him as he came into the club, before he could drink his first beer. He looked defiant as I approached him.

"Do you want to throw me out of the club? I've been a member of this club longer than you."

"I want to offer you some advice."

"I don't want any advice."

"Then you know the rules." I was seeing this conversation going in a wrong direction. "When you joined the club, you must have read the rules and accepted them."

"I live by my own rules — since I was born my life has been filled with rules and I obey them or ignore them as the whim takes me. I joined this club a long time ago and don't remember the rules. I don't like rules."

I tried a more conciliatory approach, "I don't want to discuss rules, just what happened the other night with you trying to fight."

"Trying to fight is right, those cowards would not fight me; nobody tells me to go home."

Our conversation cooled down a little and I tried to explain that he should take a conciliatory approach and pointed out that no fight had taken place. He should apologise for his bad language and behaviour and explain that he had been insulted first and it was just tit for tat. Johnny listened and agreed. I was surprised and I said so. His reply was that he didn't care for himself but he cared for Ivy and their child. We shook hands and he left after one beer.

Our committee was a mixed bunch, two Brits, one Lebanese, one Syrian and four Nigerians; our American treasurer was absent from the meeting. Johnny was called after I read the complaint and he was apologetic and said all the right things. We let him go and asked him to wait outside for our verdict — that was a mistake.

The committee was divided on what to do and the chairman decided we should discuss other business before a final decision. I wanted a quick decision but was overruled. The meeting was going for about two hours when Johnny burst into the room; he had obviously consumed a few beers. "I thought you f...ing bunch were going to give me a decision. You are all a load of f...ing cowards."

We all sat there in disbelief but before we could protest Ivy walked into the room and pulled Johnny out. A decision was immediately reached and Johnny was banned for six months. I pleaded for Ivy and her daughter to be exempt and it was agreed that only Johnny would be banned. A few days later I contacted Ivy and told her of the committee's decision and that she and her daughter were welcome at the club.

She looked me in the eye and with a wry smile said "if Johnny is not welcome here, then we are not welcome."

I don't remember seeing them in the club again.

Ibadan

John was on his way to a school leaving party for the boys' and girls' grammar schools. This was organised by the schools at the Blue Gates pub in Smethwick. They had an upstairs room for functions and there was a flat fee for a three-course meal. John was hoping he would see a girl he fancied. As he approached the bus stop, he realised he didn't have his keys so he returned home. Returning to the bus stop he had missed his bus and had to wait for the next. When he eventually arrived at the venue, everyone was seated and there was only one seat. This seat was next to a girl who was possibly the least attractive present. John thought she was a little overweight. He sat down and introduced himself as John. She was a bit surprised but said her name was Emily.

John decided to engage Emily in discussion so he explained to her he had enough A-level subjects to go to university but that he had decided to go to work. He had had part-time jobs since he was nine years old and was used to having money in his pocket. Emily explained she was leaving school a year early as she had taken her A-levels and had a scholarship to Birmingham University to study biology. So he was eighteen and she was seventeen. They joked about the age difference, then John told a joke and they were both laughing. John looked over towards Julie, the girl who he wanted to sit near. She looked bored and her male company (both sides) were trying to get her attention.

John was actually having a good time and thought he should take Emily home. After a long walk they reached Emily's home and John gave her a peck on the cheek.

"How about a proper kiss?"

John was taken aback but they had a long kiss on the lips. It was a good kiss and John asked whether she would like to go to the pictures on Sunday afternoon.

"Yes please."

"I'll pick you up here and we can stroll to the Gaumont." (This was in Smethwick). "Maybe we can have a drink in a local pub after the film."

It was all settled and as John had a long walk home, he had a lot to think about. That was not a bad evening and that kiss was worth another. As they kissed, he had felt her body against his and that was pleasurable. He had enjoyed Julie not having such a good time.

In the cinema he put his arm around Emily and felt her move closer to him. She enjoyed the film but disliked the smoke. Neither of them smoked but it seemed everyone else did. In the pub John said she should just pretend to be over eighteen. She said she only wanted a soft drink and they both laughed. Arriving at her house the second kiss was as good as the first and as her body pressed against his he became aroused.

"We don't just have to kiss."

John was shocked and took a step back.

"We're too young; if we had a baby, it could spoil our lives."

"I was not exactly thinking that far but I'm not against that proposition."

"Let's talk about it on our next date."

As he walked home, he regretted not having a condom but this affiliation was not meant to last, although he was interested in Emily. After a couple more dates John started work and Emily went to university and they drifted apart. He then started to date Julie but admitted to himself that the conversations were not too good and the kisses didn't have the same passion.

John was working four days a week and going to Warley Technical College for one day a week studying chemistry. He also had to go to night school three times a week. He started courting Julie but she liked coffee bars whereas he liked pubs. They were separated for a short time when he wanted to go to a jazz concert and she wanted to go dancing. However, John found the compromise at a place called the Res where he could hear decent music and they could dance.

The final part of his degree course could be taken either full time or part-time, two years. His company sent him full time on full pay which at the time he regarded as generous.

Julie had a wedding planned whether or not he graduated. He did graduate and went back to work but was disappointed with the raise he received. He now had a degree and had only received a raise of two hundred pounds a year. With the wedding fast approaching he was cautious about changing jobs but he put out a few feelers. One of his friends had received a scholarship to do a postgraduate degree at Nottingham University. John thought he would like university life, and so applied to a few. To his joy he was accepted at the University of London at Queen Mary College in the east end of London. Julie was keen to live in London and although the salary was not great, if Julie got a job, they would be okay. They had to live in Ilford as the rents were cheaper than in London. There was a good train and bus service to London and they went at least once a week to the West End. They tried a few restaurants, Julie liked Chinese, disliked Indian and Italian (the spaghetti was too difficult to eat), and when she saw rare beef in a German restaurant she vowed never to go there again. John went several times on his own as he loved jugged hare. He also went with his lab mates for cheap lunches at an Indian restaurant.

When John graduated, they went back to Birmingham while John was looking for a job. There was a dearth of academic jobs and John was contemplating a job in industry when an offer came from the University of Ibadan. Neither of them knew anything about Nigeria but Julie wanted to go anywhere to get out of living with their parents. They went to Nigeria, but within two months Julie had returned to the UK. When John returned for his leave Julie was with another man and wanted a divorce. John said she could have a divorce as long as she admitted to adultery, he was just anxious to get back to Ibadan.

John had been hired as a lecturer and besides his Nigerian salary he had a tax-free supplement from the British Government. When Nigeria became independent in 1960 a lot of British civil servants left and the British Government were keen to help the education system. Jeff returned to Nigeria and was promoted to senior lecturer, as the dean and vice chancellor were very pleased with his work. That meant an increase in salary, and with his supplement, he was well pleased.

The academic year passed quickly. He was a popular lecturer, and having set up his lab, was contemplating taking a post-graduate student the following year. He could go on leave for nearly three months, but was thinking of staying in England for about a month.

After a few days leave he was on the verge of cutting his leave short, when one day he went to the Smethwick market in Windmill Lane. He was looking at the vegetable stalls when he spotted a lady he knew.

"Are you Emily?"

"I certainly am, John. You've saved me the problem of finding you. I heard you were divorced and still living abroad."

"How do you know all that? And by the way you look much slimmer and it suits you?"

"Gossip is easy to come by, and thank you for the complement but there are parts of the body that are resistant to slimming. I did drop two dress sizes, though."

"No comment on that last remark, let's go to the pub across the road and have a chat." John had no idea of women's dress sizes.

"That is the one you took me to last time but this time it will cost you a glass of wine."

They sat and chatted for a while and John suggested they meet the next day and go for a meal. Emily said she was working at the Birmingham College of Advanced Technology but that they could meet in the city.

"I did the final year of my degree there and I'll come and get you, I would love to see the place again. What kind of food do you like?"

"I like Indian food but I can eat anything."

"That's great. I love Indian, so it's a date."

John escorted Emily home and received one of those delicious kisses. He was now rethinking his plans. The next day he caught a bus to the city and wandered to the college. He found his way to the biology department and knocked on Emily's office door. Emily almost dragged him into the office, shut the door and gave him a long kiss. Her body pressing against him was getting him aroused. She realised but didn't seem to mind. The meal at an Indian restaurant Emily knew, was the best he had enjoyed in years — and the company helped.

"Could you get a week off work in the next month, I could hire a car and we could go somewhere?"

"We could go next week, term is over and exam marking has finished and I'm on vacation."

John hired a car and picked up Emily at her home. As she entered the car, she put her hand in front of his face.

"Do you see anything?"

"It looks like you have a gold ring on your finger. It looks like we are married."

"Yes, I borrowed my grandmother's wedding ring from my mother, so there are no questions when we stay at a hotel."

"Shall we go to Wales? I thought we could go to Aberystwyth and make that our base."

"We can go anywhere you want, you're in charge."

They found a hotel with a vacancy and checked in as Mr. and Mrs. (they could have checked in as Dr. and Dr.). As soon as they entered the room Emily was all over him.

"Slow down a bit, Emily, we have all week."

"I can't, I've waited for this a long time and I wanted my first time to be with the man I love."

John hardly had time to get his condom on. Penetration was a bit difficult at first but once inside they both enjoyed the sensation. Intercourse later that evening was less frenetic and possibly more enjoyable. In the evening they were fully undressed and enjoying each other's bodies. Sleeping together was a bit of a problem at first until they found the correct positions. In the morning John had to find another condom and so they slept in late and missed breakfast. John decided they would have a short drive and they ended up in Borth. Emily said they should hire a couple of deckchairs and sit on the beach. John felt relaxed and asked if Emily wanted to hear about Julie — he thought he might be treading on quicksand.

"No problem, she has her life and now I want to know all you can tell me."

"After I obtained my degree, we were married, Julie had a job she disliked and my employer only offered a small raise and I now had a degree. My degree was a professional degree. I was a Graduate of the Royal Institute of Chemistry, Grad.R.I.C. One of my friends had obtained a scholarship to do a postgraduate degree at Nottingham University; I decided to apply for similar positions. I had an offer from the University of London at Queen Mary College in the east end of London. Julie wanted to live in London; we ended up in Ilford, cheaper rents.

"Ilford had a good train service to the West End, and after Julie found employment, we would go to the city at least once a week. We saw a few shows and visited a lot of restaurants and pubs. She liked Chinese food, hated Indian and Italian (the spaghetti was too difficult to eat). I took her to a German restaurant and when she saw slices of roast beef with blood in the middle we never returned. I went there on my own several times as I love jugged hare.

"After I graduated, we headed back to Birmingham; that was a disappointment for Julie. I was trying to get a job in academia and they were very scarce. Living with our parents was driving Julie nuts and when I received an offer from Ibadan University (my Professor was an external examiner) we jumped at it. All was well until we reached Heathrow to check in for our flight. There was a huge crowd at the Nigerian Airways' desk. When we finally reached the desk, the lady checking us in gave a sigh.

"'Do you have any excess baggage, can I see your on-board luggage? You are the first passengers I can check in without a hassle. I hate this desk and avoid it if I can. These people have no conception of hand baggage and paying for excess baggage. After one hour at this desk, I ask for a replacement.'

"Julie was not happy and the flight didn't improve her mood. The food was terrible and every passenger seemed to be talking loudly. Arriving in Lagos was a shock, even for me, I thought I was prepared for the heat but I didn't factor in the humidity. Descending from the plane was a shock on the system and then we entered a place referred to by Julie as a shed. Customs and Immigration were quite efficient but the heat frays nerves. Finally, we were met by a driver who took us to a hotel; he explained he would not drive to Ibadan after dark. Julie asked about a horrible smell and the driver explained it was the open sewers. I looked at Julie and I swear she turned colour. Our room was air conditioned but the evening meal was only just edible. The breakfast was worse, the eggs were swimming in oil and the sausages were like bullets. The drive to Ibadan was scary even for me. Our driver was cautious but most of the lorry drivers I would class as maniacs. We were given a flat on the third floor of a building in the university compound; it was not too well furnished and had no air conditioning only ceiling fans. There was a club with a swimming pool but Julie couldn't work. She was bored and left after two months. I had to tell the dean her mother was sick to get a ticket. Nigerians are very sympathetic when it comes to sick parents. In a way it was a relief, constant complaints can wear you down."

"Did you think of leaving with Julie?"

"No, I had a contract and for me Ibadan was as good as anywhere else. Tell me your storey."

"I was sitting at that dinner at the Blue Gates thinking: What am I doing here? Most of my friends had left school at sixteen but I was determined to do my A-levels in one year, so I was out of step with the other girls. All year it was study, study and eat, eat. Of course

47

I put on weight and when you sat next to me I was surprised."

John didn't mention it was the only seat.

"I enjoyed our chat and laughing at your jokes. When I looked around others didn't seem to be having a good time. That first kiss sealed it for me, you were the man I wanted. When I went to university and you went to work, I determined to get my degree and find you. I went to Birmingham to study biology; I was the youngest in my class. I had a couple of boyfriends but they were hopeless and I gave up on men. After my degree I found that you were already married or planning to get married. I then did a postgraduate degree specialising in botany. I graduated and looked for a job. I was offered a lectureship at Birmingham College. It was convenient as I could live at home. It was probably a mistake as I think my head of department doesn't like me. Many of the mature students are older than me and I speak my mind."

"I had noticed."

"I'm considering looking for another job."

"Give me your CV and I'll talk to our dean about offering you a job; no promises, but the dean likes me. If you get a job, you'll have to talk to our local witch doctor.

"Are you joking?"

"No, I'm very serious, this man has a good knowledge of local vegetation and makes medicines from most of them. I was introduced to him by one of my students when we were discussing metal salts used in medicine. I was very sceptical until I met the man. He spoke English very well and welcomed me. He is about sixtyish so was born about 1900. He went to an English school and learned to read and write. People would come to him to read or write letters. His customers started to tell him about their problems and most of them were anxiety related. He consulted an old witch doctor who showed him how to make potions. Most were sedatives or pain killers but he had learnt that most of his customers needed anti-depressants; he calls them coolers or "slowers". Now children are learning to read and write but some of the old folk, do not like their scrawl. They come to him to write letters. He has two types of writing, one with each letter with a small space from the next and then there is copperplate writing. He showed me and I was knocked out."

Emily leaned over to give John a kiss and the deckchair collapsed. They both had a good laugh. Near the end of the week John had run out of condoms and had to seek a fresh supply. Emily had suggested unprotected sex but John resisted. John asked whether she would like to go to a jazz concert as in the next week Chris Barber's band would be in Smethwick; Emily was all for it. John was thinking of all of the differences between this lady and Julie. Emily was his ideal partner and he had found her after too many years, but maybe she had found him. He thought, who cares she was the one for him.

Emily was in tears when he left for Nigeria but she promised to write letters, and he promised to give her CV to the dean. Within the first month he had six letters and he had only written two. At the end of the second month, he had six more but the last one was important. Emily had been offered a senior lecturer position with a tax-free British Government supplement. Of course she accepted and would be there as soon as the formalities such as a visa were completed. Now John had something to write. He was not sure how good the library was for botany texts but she should bring a couple of new text books. Each year, when he went to England John always picked up the latest chemistry text books.

John was so happy; he consulted his witch doctor friend. He told him there was a female botanist coming and would it be alright to bring her to see him. No problem, he would be happy to meet someone who knew about plants. John approached the dean about accommodation. The dean told him he was lucky because the occupant of the flat below his was off to the US. The dean enquired why he was interested in this lady.

"She is an old friend from high school. We lost touch for many years but we have renewed our friendship. She is very bright and we have had lots of discussions about collaborating in research."

The dean seemed satisfied and said he looked forward to meeting her. He did have a smile on his face.

John was so anxious for Emily to arrive. He had never noticed his loneliness but now he realised he had few friends and put all his time into work. He also realised that Emily had given his life a shake and he loved her for that. He was not only missing the physical side of their relationship, but having someone to hold a decent conversation with was probably more important. Although he had a maid to do his cleaning, washing and ironing, he was pretty untidy. His ironed shirts were just packed away in his closet and his trousers were hanging almost anyway in his wardrobe. He started to tidy his clothes, he didn't want Emily to see him as a slob; he must be in love.

When Emily's arrival time was known he arranged to go with the driver to Lagos. He had a booking at the airport hotel for which he would pay. His last letter to Emily warned her of Nigerian Airways, Lagos Airport and the heat and humidity. He had visited the flat below his and had his maid do the cleaning. He was sure he was missing something but he could think of nothing else to do.

At the airport he was watching the arrivals board which seemed to be a manual one. The flight was late but it was coming. The driver said he would wait outside and guard the car. That pleased John as he could meet her alone. Finally, he watched the plane land and his heart was in his mouth and he only relaxed when the plane came to the terminal. It took a while for Emily to emerge but when she did, she ran to John and gave him a big kiss. John was glad the driver was with the car.

"The flight was not that bad as they were over-booked and bumped me up to business class. The food was probably better than economy but not too good. One stewardess was excellent, she spoke very good English and told me about Ibadan where she was born. The airport and customs hall leave a lot to be desired and I thought I was prepared for the heat, big mistake."

They checked into the hotel and John carried her bags to the room although a porter wanted to do it. The room was hot and humid so they switched on the air conditioner and went to John's room which was the same.

"Let's go to the bar and when we return the rooms will be cool. We have to celebrate your arrival. I wanted to meet you with flowers but I couldn't find any."

"That's no problem I don't like cut flowers and all I wanted to see was you. This bar is so cool but I want to go back to my room soon I need a shower and close contact."

They finished their drinks and went to Emily's room where she started to undress after a long kiss'

"I'll go and change while you shower."

"Why not get some clean clothes and come back, then we can shower together."

As he walked back to his room all he could think about was how she was so much smarter than him. A quick shower and a lot of physical activity and they were ready for dinner.

"I'm not sure what to order but the soup is edible and the corned beef is probably imported. Be careful with the salad, particularly any raw vegetables."

"Yes, Dad."

"You realise I'm trying to protect the one I love although she is only one year younger than me. I have had amoebae dysentery as well as malaria and would not like to see the one I love suffer."

"I'm very sorry for being so flippant, of course I'll take your advice, and actually I love it when you are taking care of me."

John was so glad the rooms were air conditioned as their activity was vigorous, but the flats only had fans. The next morning at breakfast they only had toast with orange marmalade and coffee. Emily liked the coffee and John explained it was probably Nigerian, from the east. There were a few rumblings in the east but they were in the middle of Yoruba land and would not expect any problems.

The drive to Ibadan was uneventful except for the potential carnage on the road. John pointed out many wrecks on the side of the road and the ones he missed the driver showed them. Just before they entered Ibadan John asked the driver to stop and pull over. They exited the car on the crest of a hill and stood by the side of the road. Emily was glad to stretch her legs.

"Look down on the city and what do you see?"

"I see mainly bungalows with tin roofs."

"Yes, rusty tin roofs, I call this rusty city and there are very few buildings more than one storey and we'll be living in one."

"I like the idea of living with you."

"You'll be living under me."

"I like that idea better."

They reached the apartment block and John and the driver carried the luggage to the second floor. John had a key, and as they entered Emily liked what she saw. John said she should not complain if she heard noises from the flat above.

"Well pity the poor bugger in the flat below if we do it here. I think it's cooler here and I'm enjoying this place already."

John took her to see the dean and the head of biology. They were very welcoming and the head of biology was very pleased as he had no experienced staff to teach her subject. Emily asked for a curriculum and said she was prepared to lecture the next day. The dean said that was not necessary and one week should be taken to settle in and acclimatise. When he went to London, he had needed a month to acclimatise.

"This reception is more than I could expect. If the head is as good as he seems I'm going to love my job."

"Let's go back to my flat and celebrate with a couple of beers or maybe in your case a glass of white wine. It will be dark soon"

"No, I'll try a cold beer I feel thirsty. The vegetation is so lush around here I must explore. I know it gets dark soon and so quickly. I'll try to acclimatise."

"Firstly, do not go out after dark and that lush vegetation is full of insects and snakes. My witch doctor friend will tell you of the dangers but stay in the uni compound."

"Yes, Dad."

"I think the record has stuck."

The next day he took her to see his witch doctor friend and they had a long discussion about local plants. She admitted her lack of knowledge about tropical plants but she had brought some books on the subject. John had brought three beers and they relaxed. Emily asked about the doctor's patients.

"They vary but most have some anxiety and it can be something simple or if ju-ju is concerned it can be more difficult. I'll give you two examples: An old woman came and said she was losing her memory, but what worried her most was that she often forgot the names of her grandchildren. So in my best copper plate writing I wrote her name at the top of the page and the names of her grandchildren underneath. She had to go away a couple of times to ask her son for the names she had forgotten. She was so pleased and I think she must have shown it to her neighbours because I had several requests to do the same.

"In the second case a man believed one of his neighbours had put a curse on him. Ju-ju works when you believe in it and this man was suicidal. I gave him a sleeping potion and told him to come back the next day after a good sleep. The next day I hypnotised him and told him that God would punish the curser for harming him. I woke him and gave him another potion. He came back the next day and we went through the same procedure and I told him to let God punish the man. On the third day he was a changed man; he had eaten food and was happy. I have had cases that were more difficult, however, and one man I sent to a mental hospital. I provide a service mainly to the old and middle-aged. I also treat sores, ulcers and wounds, but serious cases I send to the hospital where the doctors know me. I can also set broken bones. When you come next, I'll have some plants for you but at present I'm low as I have not been harvesting for a while."

They finished their beers, thanked him and left.

"That was fascinating, I was very impressed. I just loved the way he talked with both confidence and humility. Finding him comes second to finding you. As you said, he's probably in his sixties. Next time I would like to talk to him about his culture, and his life since he was born."

"I knew you would be impressed, I'm sure he could be more than he is but he seems satisfied with his life. Now let's go to my lab and then your office. You should meet the lecturers in your department and of course see where your department resides. I have not taken a graduate student yet but if we can get a research programme going, I have an ideal candidate."

The next few weeks went very smoothly and then John plucked up the courage to ask Emily to marry him. His divorce had come through and he was a free man. Emily had no hesitation in saying yes. But how to go about it?

"We'll have a civil ceremony here, and then a church wedding if you want, when we go on leave. I think the procedure is much the same here as in England: we post banns and then four weeks later we can be married. I'll look into the formalities."

"Once we're married there is no need for a second ceremony, we can just have a party. We can go on honeymoon to Aberystwyth."

"Aberystwyth again? We've been there."

"Yes, but that is a sacred place where I lost my virginity and I want to lose it again without a condom."

The doctor had supplied three plants, two for sedatives and the third was a pain killer. Emily had examined them under the microscope and taken photos with her camera through the microscope. She had dissected them and planted some to grow more. She was very happy. Meanwhile John had set his student using the doctor's methods to extract the active ingredients. He was using more normal extraction procedures to see if the methods matched.

The wedding was a quiet one with the dean and the head of biology in attendance. There were also two

English doctors from the university hospital. Emily had visited the hospital to see the facilities. The dean had a vacated flat, but it was no surprise to him. The head of biology was pleased with anything Emily did, she was leading the department. He was particularly impressed with their research effort; it included local plants and a local doctor. He asked Emily whether he could meet this doctor. Emily asked their friend if it was okay, and he said he had no objections.

"I have just had a magical hour, I never knew this man existed, you found a very interesting fellow of my tribe,"

"Actually, John found him, he is a fund of knowledge, and besides plants he has told me about tribalism and the power of the chiefs."

"Well, you probably know, more than me, I went to an English school and then to university in England, where I spent many years. It was the climate that forced me back here."

Emily told John that if her current boss had been the man in charge at Birmingham College, she would not have left.

John was doing various chromatographic procedures on the plant extracts and finding they were complex mixtures. They had enlisted a microbiologist to test some of the extracts but they needed more sophisticated chemical instrumentation not available in Ibadan. John wanted to take some of the purified products to England when they went on leave. One day he was talking to his student about a new form of chromatography.

"Are you telling me everything you know?"

"Not only am I telling you all I know, but where I don't know I'm making educated guesses."

"My elder brother would not tell me all he knew; otherwise, he had no power over me."

"I don't have a brother, but if I did, I would have no secrets from him."

As their summer leave approached, they talked about what to do in England. Their marriage had been welcomed by Emily's family but John's parents had been less enthusiastic. John wanted a place of his own but he wanted to go to London and Aberystwyth, and how could they get a mortgage? Emily agreed that a house was a good idea but she also wanted a good time and would love to see some places in Europe. Their tax-free salaries in England had not been touched and they would have their Nigerian salaries so they were not short of money. They could spend a lot if they spent three months in England. John was for having a planned trip; Emily would do anything he planned.

"As we're landing in London let's stay in a hotel and I'll talk to some people I know and see what we can do with these samples. Then we'll go to Birmingham and look for a house and see about a mortgage. We can go to Aberystwyth for a week. Then we can go to Greece for a short holiday before returning to Nigeria."

"Yes, Dad."

"I should take you over my knee and spank you."

"Yes please."

The visit to Queen Mary College was a success as they would use a new technique called NMR (Nuclear Magnetic Resonance) and Mass Spectrometry on the samples. John would collect the results when they returned from Aberystwyth.

Their trip to Birmingham was eventful, the houses were more expensive than they had expected, and obtaining a mortgage was not so easy. Most people had stable jobs for life, but Emily and John worked abroad on contract. The banks would not touch them, but finally a building society was willing to make the gamble. They used a bit more on the deposit than they planned but they had a three-bedroom bungalow in Halesowen. Living with Emily's parents was not so bad. Her mother was very pleased that they were married and that her daughter was happy. John's parents still liked Julie and were a bit cold towards Emily. John decided not to have a party and just have a honeymoon.

Emily picked up the local gossip from a friend and found that Julie was still single. She didn't tell John as it might seem like gloating. Aberystwyth was heaven for Emily; it was the same hotel but unfortunately not the same room. The pleasure was the same and John was still as good as before. Their house needed furnishing but they decided to leave it to the following year. Emily would give her mother the key and if she saw any cut-price furniture, she should buy it and Emily would reimburse her.

The trip to Greece was interesting; John had organised that they could catch Nigerian Airways in Cairo. They landed in Athens and took a ship from Piraeus to Crete. This was the first time they had been on a boat overnight. John had booked a cabin and Emily wanted to know if they could get into the rocking rhythm of the ship. John had hired a car and they saw as much as the island as roads would allow. This was a relaxing time and at one place they booked into a hotel to be told there was a wedding on that evening, and they were welcome to sit in the restaurant and observe the festivities. As the singing and dancing was going on John looked at Emily and regretted not having a celebration of their wedding.

They both wanted to see Cairo but all they could do was change planes. They decided that next year Cairo was a place to see.

Back in Ibadan John received the results from London; they had not been ready before they went to Greece. They were complex mixtures but these results meant that they could publish a scientific article. The head of biology was so excited when he found out about the article. The authors were Emily, John his student and the microbiologist with thanks to QMC and their doctor friend. When they showed this to their friend, he said, "I'll buy the beers."

All was going well, and then in September Emily said she was pregnant. John was now in a flap, their house in England had almost no furniture, and Emily would have to fly back on her own. Emily solved the problem by saying she was having the baby in Ibadan.

"Now you *are* joking."

"No, I have talked to the doctors and they say they can cope even if there are complications. They see hundreds of births each year and this will be no different. The hospital is clean and the nurses well trained, so I have no reservations. I'll be able to work until my eighth month and you'll be around; so no argument."

Johns only was response was "When did it happen?"

"The dirty deed could be either in Aberystwyth or Crete but I like the former. It means so much to me — I'm a sentimental girl."

Emily lectured until the doctors insisted she go into hospital. At this stage John was a nervous wreck. The birth was normal and out popped a little girl with a little bit of blonde hair. John was waiting outside when two nurses exited from the delivery room dancing and rejoicing. The doctor came out and said he had a daughter, the first white baby born in the hospital. John was a bit stunned but all the nurses were rejoicing.

John entered the room to be confronted by a beaming Emily.

"I want another baby."

"Now you *are* joking."

"Yes, that was not so bad and have you seen her?"

"No, they whisked her away to clean her and from what I hear from the nurses they may not bring her back."

"I would not have had better treatment in England, these nurses are so professional and kind. During birth all I could think of was you, and your face was everywhere I looked. My life without you would have been very different and more miserable."

The nurses returned the baby and John was apprehensive about holding such a small creature. There was a little patch of blonde hair and she was so white. The nurses called her Little Oibo. Emily told John she was to stay in hospital a couple of days to make sure there was no problem with her or the baby.

"What are we going to call her?"

"We could try Julie."

"I hope you're joking."

"Of course I am. You pick the names of our daughter and I'll pick the names of our future son."

They both had a good laugh and the baby stirred but didn't cry. John went home, had a few beers, sampled some of their duty free and had a good night's sleep. When he visited Emily the next day, she had a shopping list which included a pram and lots of nappies. He had to consult the nurses about those two items. One nurse had an uncle who could get those things. All the nurses could talk about was this little white baby with blonde hair. In the nursery they had a window to view the babies. There was a queue of visitors to see his daughter.

Emily was in good spirits and had decided on Sarah as the name for their daughter, and as a second name she had picked a Yoruba name, Bisi.

"I think it means first child but I like the name, do you agree?"

"Yes, now how about Archibald Albion for our son."

"If that is the case, I'm not having another child."

That turned out to be prophetic as they didn't have any more children.

"Did you tell our parents they are grandparents?"

"Not yet, but now I have a name I'll do so, but maybe I'll not tell them the second name, I'm not sure they'll understand."

When news got out that the baby's second name would be Bisi the nurses threw a party. As Emily and Sarah left the hospital there was a crowd of well-wishers. One of the doctors said the whole hospital was a happy place and he had never seen such a crowd for a leaving patient. John's house girl/cleaner, Mary, was anxious to be a nanny and when she saw Sarah she was overwhelmed. John was a bit surprised but Emily said she had seen a few visitors in the same state.

Emily was keen to get back to work but John was telling her to relax and so were the dean and her head of department. Emily liked the pram except on the third floor it was not so practicable. John found a little cubicle in the entrance and set up a locking system. He let it be known that if the pram was stolen Sarah would not be seen in public. That was remarkably effective, and all his neighbours and their servants would keep an eye on the pram.

Sarah was a remarkably quiet baby she hardly ever cried and John would often take a look at her to see if she was okay. Emily was much more relaxed and said that if there was a problem, she would sense she was needed. Emily had lectures in the morning and in the afternoon would often take Sarah out in the pram to the hospital. She took Mary with her to talk to well-wishers who would often crowd around the pram. The nurses were always glad to see Sarah and as she grew their interest intensified, mainly due to her mop of blonde hair.

Their vacation was approaching but Sarah was probably too young to travel. Emily decided that John should go and furnish the house. He would also take numerous photos to show the grandparents.

"If I furnish the house with furniture you hate, what will you say?"

"I'll bite my tongue and say I love what you have done. Take my mother with you when you go shopping and don't stay too long in England. I'll miss you."

John had more samples for Queen Mary College and although he would miss Emily and Sarah he had to go. He planned to spend only a couple of weeks in England but shopping took more time than he had thought. Emily's parents were very happy to see the photos but his parents seemed less enthusiastic. He spent most of his time with Emily's parents, and her father was quite talkative when John had him alone in the pub.

Roy, Emily's father, said she was a single-minded girl and she would go after anything she wanted with gusto. He was not surprised she liked Ibadan. Emily talked to her mother, but confided in her father. He knew all about John before he met him. He was worried it was an obsession but when he met John he relaxed.

Shopping with Emily's mother was not easy, he wanted to buy the first thing he saw but she made him look further. She was right but time was passing. Finally, he had some basic furniture and decided to leave. He was lucky his Nigerian flight was over-booked and he was bumped up to business class. Arriving at Lagos Airport he was surprised to be greeted by Emily.

"Where's Sarah?"

"She is with Mary who is very capable and I trust her. I couldn't wait to see you."

Life back in Ibadan was going smoothly but there were problems in the east of Nigeria. A few of the lecturers who were Ibos left the university and moved back to their homeland. Their doctor friend often talked to them about tribalism and he was following the news in the newspapers and said there would be conflict. He believed Ibadan was a safe place, but even in the Yoruba nation there were plenty of dissenting groups. John and Emily discussed the problem but decided to stay. Sarah was growing and outside the compound she was a star. Her weekly visit to the hospital had the whole place in uproar. She was a quiet child who rarely cried and would often wake with a smile on her face. John couldn't believe his luck and the nurses told him he had a special child.

The next year, when they went to England, Sarah was a great success — even with John's parents. Emily soon had their house fully furnished and said if they had to leave Nigeria she could easily settle back there. They decided to leave Cairo till the next year until Sarah was a little older. Returning to Lagos they noticed lots of troops everywhere and there were three checkpoints on the road to Ibadan.

They both started to think about staying for another year. Both John and Emily were keen to get more samples as they had collaboration with a Professor of Pharmacy in Scotland. They had written a few scientific papers and John's student had his name on more papers than some of the professors. The doctor was so proud to have his name on scientific papers and took copies of each one.

One of the English doctors at the hospital decided to leave, and at his leaving party told John to look out for a job in England. He felt the political climate in Nigeria was changing. Emily was also starting to think about Sarah's education, she would soon need to go to a nursery and later to a kindergarten. They agreed to give it one more year with Emily saying probably two years. That spurred John to use all his contacts to find a job in England, or even Scotland.

Near the end of the academic year there was a job in Wolverhampton. It would be quite a commute but John was willing to drive. They finally decided to leave and gave their notice. Their doctor friend was unhappy to see them leave, as were all the nurses in the hospital. The dean thanked them for lifting the profile of the university with their scientific papers. John's student was offered a lectureship. All the nurses at the hospital were unhappy to see them go and there was much wailing when they left.

Emily said "I suppose I won't get to see Cairo."

"Maybe in a few years when Sarah will be bigger."

"When you told me about Ibadan all I could think about was being with you, but this place has grown on me. It's not the easiest place to live but it has entered my soul. My professional career has taken off and I couldn't see that at Birmingham College. I laugh when I think about my reaction when you mentioned a witch doctor. He was a revelation and he has helped us so much, let's take a photo of the three of us and have it framed — we can present it to him."

Unfortunately, the doctor was away visiting a sick relative when they took it to his house. His wife said he would prize it and probably hang it in his office. There were many tears when they said goodbye and Emily had tears when they took off from Lagos Airport. Sarah seemed to enjoy the flight.

Back in Halesowen life was slow and the only problem was the drive to work for John. They decided to move and found a house in Wombourne a village close to Wolverhampton — a village in the country, surrounded by green fields.

Emily said, "This greenery reminds me of Ibadan and I love it."

Kano

Lionel had been in the Nigerian Civil Service, but independence had forced him out of a job and 1960 was a turning point in his career.

When WWII started Lionel was too young to be conscripted. Living in heavily bombed Coventry he was about to be sent with other children to the country but his mother forestalled that by sending him to her sister in Evesham. This country town on the River Avon was very quiet, but more importantly it was close enough so Lionel's mother could visit at the weekend.

Lionel initially had problems at school, his accent produced lots of laughter with the locals, both children and adults. The second problem was bullying in the school. Lionel was tall for his age and he soon had to fight when he saw smaller children being bullied. As his accent softened, he became more accepted. Reading and writing were not his forte but he excelled at arithmetic. His capability with numbers became useful when he left school. 1947 was not the best time to look for a job but the recommendation of his teacher found him a job in a seed company. They allowed him time to do a part-time study of book keeping. At night school he studied English so that he could improve his spelling and writing.

After the end of the war his mother wanted him to return to Coventry but he persuaded her that life in Evesham was better. When he started at the seed company he was never going to return to Coventry. He was employed in the accounts office and soon appointed to the assistant to the accounts' manager.

Lionel realised that he would go no further with this company. One of his lecturers at college suggested he take an exam to get into the civil service. He passed the exam and was sent to Glasgow to an office dealing with fisheries. The big city had no attraction for him and the work was tedious. From the very first week he was looking for another job in the service. One advert took his attention; it was basically a job for a clerk in the Nigerian Civil Service with possibilities of advancement. He applied and then consulted his parents and his aunt and uncle. The reply from his parents was very negative but his uncle had an army friend who had served in Nigeria and their reply was much more optimistic.

The Nigerian Civil Service was under the wing of the British but his aunt had no idea how much it was controlled. His uncle's friend had enjoyed his time in Lagos but the major problem was the heat and humidity. If Lionel could live with problems his uncle thought that advancement would be very possible. There were lots of perks to the job and Lionel should think about acquiring a nest egg for the future. Lionel had not been outside England except for his time in Scotland. He had not thought about travel but now he was excited about going to Africa. He had to consult atlases to find Nigeria in Africa. His school studies had been very weak on geography and it surprised him that southern Nigeria was close to the equator.

He had not been in the Glasgow office long enough to make any real friends but everyone he talked to about the new job was urging him to go. One or two of the older men said they were jealous and as younger men they would have jumped at the chance. They were all sure if it didn't work out, he would easily slip back into the British Civil Service.

Lionel waited a few weeks after submitting his application and was about to give up on the job when an invitation to an interview arrived. The interview was in Glasgow so he had no need to travel. This was an interesting interview which started by asking about his political affiliations; he had none. What did he think about colonisation? He had no thoughts. Did he know any black people? No, he had been bought up in a country town and had never met a black person. What were his thoughts about Africa? He had looked at maps and now understood how big it was.

After that series of peculiar questions, he was asked whether he had a passport. Not yet. He was advised to get one as he had the job. The process was over in less than twenty minutes and Lionel was in a daze at the end of the interview. He had not been able to ask a question, not that he had any. Returning to the office everyone was asking him questions but the only one he could positively answer was that he had the job. Several of his colleagues invited him to the pub after work to celebrate his good fortune. Most of the younger men said they would seriously look at the job vacancies in the future. The older men wished him luck and most said they wished they were younger.

Getting a passport was a formality, but telling his parents of his new job was more difficult. He had very little information; he didn't even know his salary. He assumed he was going to the capital Lagos but as yet he didn't know where he was going. He would be working for the Nigerian Civil Service but was not sure what that meant. Letters to his aunt couldn't give much information as he had none. Finally, a letter arrived with the employment conditions; the salary was generous, with free accommodation and one month's leave each year. His father was very impressed, the salary was the important point; it was more than he had received. His mother was still not happy but admitted the conditions were good. His uncle marvelled at one month's leave as most jobs in England only offered two weeks a year.

The letter regretted that he would have to travel by sea as flights were only reserved for senior personnel. Lionel had never been on a plane or a ship so he didn't care. Now he went back to the maps and realised this would be a long journey. He was now looking at all sorts of maps at the local library. He realised how little he knew about geography and with his love of numbers he started to take a serious look at distances. Comparing England, Wales and Scotland with Nigeria was a bit of a shock, he had assumed they were of similar size. Nigeria was a big country!

When he told his colleagues the salary and conditions, they were all jealous. At his leaving party he had a list of names of colleagues who wanted jobs in Nigeria. His journey to Liverpool was paid for, along with one night's accommodation. It was a chance to say goodbye to his parents, uncle and aunt. Lionel's thoughts of a big liner were squashed when he saw the freighter that was going to be his home for a while. His uncle was thoughtful and had brought him some books to read on his journey. Lionel's uncle had given him six books that all had some reference to Africa and Lionel read each one cover to cover twice.

The journey was fascinating as they docked at many ports before Lagos. Lionel got to know the captain and most of the crew; this opened his eyes to non-English speaking people. He realised his lack of language skills and hoped his job would only involve English. As they approached Lagos the crew became excited. The captain explained that Lagos was an exciting town and had lots of pleasures for the crew. Lionel was not sure what that meant but he assumed it would mean extended shore leave.

He was met at the dock, and Customs and Immigration formalities were swift and informal. He was whisked off to a hotel and told to relax for two days.

Lionel would be picked up and taken to the office at nine in the morning on the third day. All his meals had been pre-paid and he was given several pounds for incidentals. After the ship, everything seemed hot and stuffy. The bar had fans and a cold beer hit the spot. He sat at the bar and all the staff were black but very polite and friendly. He started to think about his interview. In his room he had his fan on full blast and after a while he fell asleep.

In the morning he was thirsty, very thirsty. Breakfast was not appetising and so he only had toast with jam and coffee. The area around the hotel was rather depressing. The open sewers were not pleasant and combined with the humidity Lionel was feeling nauseous. Back in the hotel a cold beer settled his stomach. He had little appetite for the evening meal, but a couple of beers sent him to bed with a good night's sleep. The next morning, he was picked up and taken to the office.

The manager was English but all the staff were Nigerian. The manager confessed that he was not sure what Lionel would do but that he should roam around the office and find out what the staff were doing. Lionel was not sure what he should do but had conversations with several clerks. Finally, he found one who was logging shipping in Lagos harbour; this interested Lionel. He asked about the ship that he had been on when he arrived in Lagos. The goods off-loaded had been logged but not the passengers; he had been a passenger but this log didn't have any information of his landing. Of course the Customs and Immigration would have a record of his landing but was he a commodity to be recorded as an import?

At the end of the working day the manager invited him to a club attached to the High Commission where he could meet other Brits. The attraction was that the evening meal could be fish and chips or roast beef and Yorkshire pudding. The manager said he would steer Lionel clear of one or two snobbish Brits who would laugh when they heard he was working for the Nigerian Civil Service. They were public school boys with more self-belief than common sense.

The evening was very pleasant and the fish and chips were as good as he had ever tasted in either England or Scotland. He had a chat with the consul and was really impressed. This man was ex-army and had served in several countries; his stories were spellbinding. One fellow was from Stratford and knew Evesham well and that was a good chat. The beer was cheap and Lionel had to restrain himself not to get drunk.

The next day Lionel was informed he would be going to Kano, capital of North Nigeria. The office there was smaller than the Lagos office but the manager was nearing retirement and there was a good chance that Lionel could get his job. Kano was not a popular posting. A compensation of this posting was that Kano was much dryer than Lagos but it could be hotter.

Lionel's head was spinning, he had been in Nigeria for only a few days and already there was talk of promotion. The good news was that he would fly to Kano. The Lagos manager invited him to the army surplus store to pick out some items he might need for his new job. The manager joked that they might claim the cost of these items back, but he would write them off.

Lionel was surprised at the items available, shorts, sandals and short sleeves shirts were the first items to be picked. A shaving kit with shaving soap, hairbrush and comb were obvious choices. He then spied a pair of binoculars, they could come in useful. Lionel was feeling a bit uncomfortable but the manager said these items might be thrown out at some later date so not to worry. There was a beautiful knife which he picked and would have loved a sword but thought that would not be acceptable. There was a pith helmet which he couldn't resist. Finally, he had a kit bag that would accommodate his new acquisitions.

Now he was going to take his first flight and he was nervous. Climbing the steps to the plane he had a funny feeling that made him look at the tarmac and hope he would see it again. He closed his eyes at take-off and then couldn't take his eyes off the world below. The plane was only half full and he had a window seat. He was fascinated with the changing scenery and as they approached Kano there was a lot of desert. Landing was smooth but descending from the plane he had to shield his eyes from the sand blowing across the airport.

Lionel was excited but apprehensive about his new position; it was happening so fast. What was this new job? Why was Kano important? What could he do?

He was met at the airport by a young man who was going to be Lionel's right-hand man. Ahmed had been to English school and was not much older than Lionel; he explained his job as helping Lionel with Hausa. They went to the office where Lionel was introduced to the manager and the staff. The staff all rose and bowed, then Lionel said he was glad to be in Kano. Ahmed translated and then the office descended into applause.

The manager, Archie, admitted that he was soon going to retire and that if Lionel was to stay in Kano, he would be an obvious replacement. He warned Lionel that there was no night life in Kano and only a small club. There were very few expatriates and there was a continual turnover. He could only name three Brits who had stayed in Kano more than five years. Kano was a trading centre and Lionel should concentrate on understanding and cataloguing trade.

Lionel was provided with a furnished two-bedroom flat and a man servant to look after his needs. All rooms had ceiling fans and the flat was on the second floor. Ahmed thought it was wise to be on the second floor, as although robberies were rare, it was unlikely they would venture to the second floor. Lionel immediately liked Ahmed as he was thinking of Lionel's wellbeing.

Archie took Lionel to the club and enrolled him as a member. His fees were paid for by his employer.

Archie had convinced his superiors in Lagos that this multicultural expatriate membership was a good place to learn about trade in Kano. Archie advised that many of the long-term expatriates were traders from the Middle East and their knowledge of Arabic helped them in their trade. Archie was the treasurer of the club and Lionel's knowledge should make him the next treasurer.

Lionel was settling well into the job, and Ahmed was answering most of his questions and seemed enthusiastic about some of Lionel's thoughts. Lionel wanted to learn some basic Hausa and they spent two days in the office going through some basic phrases. Lionel admitted he was having difficulty, this language was very different to his school-boy French. Ahmed smiled and said Lionel would slowly absorb the language and Ahmed would earn his money by being a translator. Lionel liked this man more and more but wondered how much Hausa he could absorb.

After a few days in the office Lionel wanted to visit the markets. Ahmed explained there were three markets, the vegetable market which merged with the meat market, and then the cattle market.

"We'll walk through all the markets, I'll smile and nod but say nothing. You should listen to what the people say. You can make replies where necessary but when we return to the office you can tell me what they say."

"Can I say you'll be a future Archie?"

"Yes, but that may not turn out to be true."

What Lionel didn't know was that Ahmed was the nephew of one of the Emirs. Archie knew but had neglected to tell Lionel — as instructed. Ahmed told his uncle of the market tour. All the market people were talking about Lionel — they were confused. Lionel then called all the vegetable stall holders to a meeting and when they arrived there was a long rectangular table with water jugs and cut lemons and oranges on the table. There seemed to be a bit of an argument about seating. Finally, when they were all seated Lionel started to ask questions through Ahmed. After a short period, Lionel stopped the proceedings, picked up his chair and moved to the opposite end of the table. A little time later he picked up his chair and moved to the middle of the table. After the meeting, Lionel explained to Ahmed he wanted them to realise they were all equal. On hearing this strategy, the Emir laughed out loud.

"I couldn't do that but I like the concept."

The meeting with the butchers and the cattle traders followed the same pattern but there was no problem with the initial seating. Word had spread of this eccentric Englishman.

Lionel had lots of answers to his questions about where produce coming into Kano was from. The next question was the goods leaving Kano and how to quantify the answers. Lionel's forte was numbers. Ahmed informed him there was another part of the trade, the Bedouin.

Lionel had read about the Bedouin during his readings in the Glasgow Library. He only knew they were nomads who roamed over the deserts in North Africa using camels. Ahmed explained they were often family groups that would bring goods from as far as Sudan and Morocco. Family groups could speak their own language which was generally a corruption of Arabic and there could be a mix of Berber and Arabic. Ahmed admitted he could only talk to them in Arabic but they were generally hospitable. He also said that if they visited their camp the women would go into hiding. When a group camped outside Kano, he would let Lionel know, they rarely came into the city.

Lionel realised he had seen very few women during his short time in Kano. Ahmed explained that Hausa women would not go to the market and if there was a woman in the market she would be from southern Nigeria. Hausa women could be seen going to and coming from the mosque on Friday. The only women Lionel was seeing were wives of members at the club.

Lionel started to collect data of the trade being carried out in Kano. The fruit and vegetable trade were mainly a local trade with very few middle men. The farmers were bringing their produce to market. Lionel set up a good rapport with these traders. Other commodities such as plastic ware were controlled by middlemen, some were expatriates, members of the club. The meat market was more complicated. Cattle were moving over most of northern Nigeria, some of the cattle were moved over 1000 miles to market. Southern Nigeria had the tsetse fly and so the better cattle came from northern Nigeria, the patterns of the meat and cattle markets were more difficult to quantify. Lionel loved these problems.

Ahmed informed Lionel that a Bedouin group were camped about five miles from Kano. The local traders would be visiting them for the next few days. Lionel and Ahmed went to the camp and met the chief. He wanted to trade but they explained they wanted to know where he came from and where he was going. His attitude became a little bit frosty but he did tell them he had come from Omdurman in the Sudan and would be going west. He would give no information on the size of his group only that they had many camels and goats. Ahmed told Lionel that if they had goats, they would not go deep into the desert. Lionel thought long and hard how the next meeting could be more useful.

Lionel wrote regularly to his parents and his aunt and uncle and told them how he liked Kano. His mother kept asking when he was coming home and his uncle was reminding him of his nest egg. Lionel was only spending a small portion of his salary, and most of it was going back to his bank in England. At times he thought about some female company but although there was little prostitution in Kano, he rejected trying the women on offer. He had minimal contact with women, only the married ladies in the club.

In one of his letters, he wrote about the Bedouin, and his uncle had a suggestion. Why not give the chief a present? Lionel discussed this with Ahmed. What could he give a Bedouin chief? Looking through his possessions he settled on the binoculars he had received in Lagos. He had not used them and he could always get a replacement. The binoculars were in a leather case but they were not new and looked quite old.

The returning Bedouin group had been as far as Algeria and had many items to trade. Lionel and Ahmed were welcomed and the chief was presented with the binoculars. Lionel explained that his present had belonged to a British officer who had died many years ago. The chief smelled the case, it was not camel or goat shin. Ahmed explained it was very old cattle skin and probably had no smell. The chief corrected him, he could smell the leather. Lionel was starting to think the present was a mistake. Ahmed showed the chief how to use the binoculars, now Lionel saw real pleasure. The chief was walking about his camp and there was lots of laughter. The chief came back and said Lionel had given him new eyes and in return Lionel would get new life. When Ahmed explained that to Lionel he frowned until a young camel was presented to Lionel. Ahmed said, "You must accept this gift and I'll find it a home."

Lionel was astounded; he had a young camel for a present that had cost him nothing. The chief promised to come back and that Lionel would be a guest of honour. The Emir told Ahmed this was a real present, camels were very precious to the Bedouin.

After one year Lionel had a month's leave and Ahmed promised to look after the office. Lionel first went to Coventry as it was close to Birmingham Airport. At home his mother talked about nothing but when was he coming back to England and his father was talking about the cost of living. He decided to go to Evesham where his aunt and uncle would be better company. His aunt and uncle were more receptive to his stories and he was a celebrity at the local pub. Everyone wanted to know about the Bedouin and the camel. The only problem was the weather; it was always cloudy and often raining. He had not really noticed clouds except in the rainy season; Kano was almost always bright and cloudless.

After two weeks he was keen to go back to Kano. He decided to spend two weeks in Crete to see the sun. Lionel picked Crete after a fantastic night in the club. He had met an Australian archaeologist who was visiting for a few days and he was told stories about the war. Bruce was in the army and had fought in Greece then evacuated to Crete and then evacuated to Egypt. His time in those countries had made up his mind to become an archaeologist. One night Lionel had introduced Bruce to a Greek member and this was the best night he had spent in the club. It was a night with lots of drinks, much talk about Greece and Crete, ending with the Australian and Greek in a long hug. Lionel had said almost nothing except in introduction but now he was fascinated with ancient history. Bruce had gone north to Niger and Chad but Lionel had invited him to stay any time he was in Kano.

Within the next few years Archie retired. Lionel had asked Archie whether he could name his camel, Archie. They had agreed but there was a problem, the camel was female. Lionel took Archie's job but he still loved to go out into the field particularly to meet the Bedouin.

He had become president and treasurer of the club and had welcomed Bruce several times. On his leave he would spend one week in England and the rest of the time in Crete and Cairo. He had the ideal job he loved and had plenty of leisure time. He had no female company but he became used to that. He was now in contact with several Bedouin tribes and had raided the army stores for presents. A couple of the army officers were members of the club and they found him old army surplus.

The only problem for Lionel was the approaching independence. He was working for the Nigerian Civil Service and he was certain he couldn't retain his position. Not long after the independence celebrations there was a total reorganisation of the service. He was made redundant and he was not yet thirty. His settlement was generous and his job was going to Ahmed.

Ahmed said that the Emir would like to see Lionel. Lionel had met the Emir several times but had never been summoned to a meeting. He was thinking what to do next when the Emir offered him a job. Ahmed always had Lionel thinking he had some way to get to the Emir but had not suspected he was the Emir's nephew. His camel was being taken care of in the Emir's farm and the Emir had watched his every move since arriving in Kano.

The Emir explained that life under this new government was uncertain for Kano and his people, but he wanted them to prosper. He wanted information on how this independence was going to affect the north of Nigeria. Lionel was to look at trade in the whole of northern Nigeria and his friendship with the Bedouin was an important component. He was also interested in keeping the Kano club running as normal as it gave Kano a special contact with foreign merchants. Lionel would get a generous salary and a two-bedroom apartment and one month's leave a year. The Emir joked he wished *he* could take one month's leave.

Lionel couldn't believe his luck, he had a job that was a mirror image of his old job but now the job had more scope. He thanked the Emir and Ahmed, he said that Ahmed had fooled him but he was happy. The Emir announced that Lionel's camel was pregnant and they should celebrate as camels were prized by his people. The Emir produced a bottle of champagne and Lionel should take it home as he and Ahmed couldn't drink alcohol.

As Lionel lay in bed that night, he couldn't believe his luck, he could stay in Kano and almost nothing had changed. His only problem was losing Ahmed as his translator. Hausa and Arabic were difficult languages and Lionel was not a linguist. As he lay in bed, he realised his new challenge was to find an assistant who spoke English, Arabic and Hausa.

The next day he consulted Ahmed and it was all sorted. Idris, his younger brother was going to be Lionel's assistant. Ahmed confided that Idris was young and might need to be watched. Lionel realised Ahmed was a true friend he had warned him about his brother. Idris turned out to be a very good assistant.

Lionel reported to the Emir quite often and they became good friends. The Emir was starting to see frictions between the south, east and north of Nigeria and he was concerned how that could be a problem for Kano. Lionel advised that they should look at the population of Kano. The Emir was in agreement, they needed to know the allegiances of the residents. Lionel also asked how long the influences of the Emirs and chiefs could last in this new country.

"You have asked me a question that I cannot answer but it worries me, ask around and let me know your thoughts."

Kano being a northern city had a mainly Hausa population with small groups of Yoruba and Ibo. There were very few foreigners, but a large group from Niger and Chad. They were all mainly traders but some of the Ibos were lawyers and quite high up in the civil service. Many of the Yoruba were officers in the army. The Hausa were mainly foot soldiers; that worried the Emir.

One day as Lionel entered the club the guard said he had a visitor. As he approached the veranda, he could see a brown-haired woman with her back to him.

"Are you Mr. Lionel? I have to see you about temporary membership, apparently. I'm Ingrid, a photographer."

"Welcome Ingrid. Would that be a single membership?"

Lionel had not meant to be so formal but he had asked the correct question. This was a very good-looking young lady and he was almost spell-bound.

"Yes, I'm single and I'll be here about one or two months. It all depends on accommodation. At the moment I'm staying in a hotel and cannot afford more than month even though it's a cheap hotel."

"I know someone who has some vacant flats and he might be able to rent one to you for a couple of months. How come you contacted me?"

"I was told by a friend in Lagos that you know the Bedouin, I want to photograph them. Secondly he recommended the club as the place to meet you."

"That must be Klaus, he was looking to invest in this area but I could never discover what he did for a living. I called him Clever Klaus. Photographing the

Bedouin may not be simple. Even photographing people in Kano may be more complicated than it would be in Europe. People in this area are conservative and many are superstitious. Would you like a soft drink?"

"No, I would prefer a beer."

"So would I. This climate is suitable to a cold beer."

Lionel was talking to Ingrid as he would to a male friend. He rarely talked to women and then when he did it was in the presence of their husbands. Ingrid explained that she was a freelance photographer and she would sell her photographs to newspapers and magazines when she returned to Germany. Lionel invited Ingrid to dinner at the club, and he was loath to let her go back to her hotel. After dinner and a couple more beers — Lionel would not let her pay — he escorted her back to her hotel. They promised to meet at the club the next afternoon.

The next day Lionel sent Idris out to investigate accommodation in Kano while he approached a man who had recently built a block of flats. He told the Emir that accommodation was important for the growth of Kano. He admitted he had an ulterior motive, a German photographer called Ingrid.

"Lionel you are an honest man, your idea about accommodation is very important and I support your study, but you have told me your motive. No one tells me their motive."

Lionel found a flat and late in the afternoon he took Ingrid to see the building. As he walked behind Ingrid, he found the sway of her hips, hypnotic. The flat was very poorly furnished but Ingrid said it would be okay. Another dinner with a couple of beers and Lionel was in love. He warned Ingrid about photographing people, and that he would have Idris show her the city. The next day in the office he couldn't concentrate on Idris's report about accommodation — all he could think about was Ingrid.

Idris had taken Ingrid to the camel farm and identified Lionel's camel. Idris told her that Lionel visited this farm every week and the camel knew him when he visited. Idris thought that the camel was pregnant but he was not sure — it was too early to know. Ingrid was very impressed with the story.

Lionel had learnt that a Bedouin group were encamped but it was a group he had only met once so they had to be careful. He asked Idris whether it would be wise to take Ingrid to the camp. Idris's advice was that they should go to talk to the leader without Ingrid. Lionel was in agreement. Lionel felt he had to take a special present to this Bedouin chief. The army garrison was now run by Nigerians but he was well known and liked by the commandant. Lionel rummaged through the army surplus and came upon an old pith helmet. This had obviously been owned by a senior officer and it was at least thirty years old.

When Lionel presented the helmet to the Bedouin chief, he explained it had belonged to a great soldier. The chief took off his turban, and the helmet was a perfect fit. Parading around the camp in his new helmet there was much merriment. The chief asked if Lionel could come back tomorrow as he had to think of a present. This gave an opportunity for Lionel to ask if he could bring a female photographer. The chief knew about photographs but no women and most males would not be photographed but children could be photographed. Lionel asked about camels. This amused the chief who said that any camel who said no would be elevated to a leader.

Lionel was really happy to tell Ingrid they could visit the Bedouin camp but there were lots of restrictions. Ingrid asked what she should wear; head to toe covering was the answer.

The next day Lionel, Idris and Ingrid went to the camp. Lionel asked Ingrid to stay by the car until they knew where she was allowed to go. The chief would not let her into his tent. She could go to the woman's tent but must take no photographs. She could go near the camels and she could take photos of the children. Idris relayed the instructions and the men retired to the chief's tent. As they sat around drinking tea the chief said that Lionel's present had caused so much laughter in the camp, he had to give a similar present. He was giving Lionel help. He introduced a young boy called Ali, he was to be Lionel's servant. Lionel was shocked but Idris said that he must accept the gift. Lionel was stunned but agreed. The chief then gave information about the boy. His father had recently died and his mother was ill. She didn't want Ali to see her die and she wanted him to become educated. Lionel was shaken but this was a very good reason to take the boy.

Ingrid was waiting by the car when Lionel, Idris and Ali emerged from the tent.

"Who is this young boy?"

"This is Ali and he is my gift."

"Are you joking?"

"No, I can't believe it myself. We're going to take him to the camel farm and I'll discuss with the Emir what we can do with him."

"Well that probably trumps what I did but I think I have some amazing shots. The visit to the women's tent was amazing, of course I couldn't understand what they said but there was continual laughter. I was expecting them to stare glumly at me but they were very welcoming. I did get a shot of one man holding a camel; he seemed okay with me taking his photograph."

"I hope you took plenty of photos of smiling children, the Bedouin seem to have a reputation as austere people but they are not."

They went straight to the camel farm and Ali was introduced to Archie but the herder informed them that Archie was a female and she was pregnant.

"I rename you Alice. Tell Ali this camel is mine and he should get to know her and he should try to say Alice."

The next day Lionel visited the Emir and told him the story of Ali.

"You gave this Bedouin a present that had a good effect in his camp and he had to reciprocate by giving you a better present. He was also giving this boy a chance at a better life. I'll see to his education but his allegiance is to you so you have to see him regularly and encourage him to learn English, he is now your son."

Lionel was thinking that he had a son and was not married. How would he explain that to his mother? He decided not to tell his parents of a new family member. That evening in the club Ingrid was excited, and she wanted to go back to the camp but Lionel advised that she should wait for the next group. Lionel told her about the advice from the Emir, and assured her that Ali would get a good education.

"Is your bathroom larger than mine?"

"Yes, why do you ask?"

"I need to set up a dark room. Could I borrow your bathroom for an afternoon? I want to see some of my shots from the camp and some others I have taken around Kano. I need a few black sheets which I've seen in the market and I have the rest of the equipment to set up a crude dark room."

"Of course. I would like to see your work."

The next day they set up the dark room in Lionel's bathroom, and Lionel left for work leaving Ingrid alone. Late in the afternoon Lionel arrived and announced his presence. Ingrid came out in her bra and pants much to Lionel's surprise and delight.

"It's so hot in there; if I do this again, I'll need a fan. Now you have seen nearly all of me and I hope you like what you see."

Lionel was speechless and just nodded in the affirmative. Ingrid went back into the dark room and Lionel poured himself a beer. A little later Ingrid reappeared and said she was finished and would dismantle the equipment and have a shower. Lionel had had his shower at the office. Finally, Ingrid emerged with a bath towel around her body.

"I'm so excited with the photographs you deserve a present."

With that she dropped the towel and she was totally naked.

"We should go to your bedroom for the present."

Lionel was speechless but he couldn't wait to lose his virginity. As they lay naked with the ceiling fan drying some of the sweat from their exertion Ingrid said that Lionel should see her photographs. Lionel was watching a naked lady bringing him photographs, he was in heaven. The photos were good and he was looking at things he looked at every day but didn't see. The photo of Ali with Alice touched him and he told Ingrid he must have that one. Ingrid was very impressed that he picked that one, Lionel was a sensitive man.

The next couple of months passed quite fast but no new Bedouin came to Kano. The dark room was only used a couple of times but Lionel's bedroom had regular use. When Ingrid left Lionel was sad but she said she would sell some of her photographs and write about Kano and the Bedouin, and then she would come back. Lionel settled back into his routine and was teaching Ali English as well as taking him to school. He was a bright boy and would often tell Lionel about nomadic life. Lionel wanted to write to his relatives about his son but he thought they may not understand. On the other hand, his letters to Ingrid were all about Ali. The letters from Ingrid were all positive; she had sold several photos and talked on the radio about Kano. Her stories about the Bedouin had been taken by German, French and English publications. She couldn't wait to get back to Kano.

Ingrid's return was a time of great joy for Lionel. Ali and Idris saw Lionel's change as Ingrid's arrival approached. Idris had taken a special interest in Ali and was helping him with his studies particularly Hausa and Arabic. Also, Alice had delivered a male camel who Lionel named Archie.

Ingrid's new flat was very close to Lionel's and it was much better furnished than her first flat. Lionel wished she could live with him but in this Moslem society that would cause a problem. Even the Emir suggested that Lionel should think about marriage.

Lionel was immersed in Ingrid and her photographs. One photo of the club was particularly good and he offered to buy it for the club.

"Lionel, I could never charge for a picture of a place I have enjoyed many times. Anyway, the going price for one of my photographs is too much. Seriously, any photographs you want are free. You have made Kano a fantastical place and you have made my time here magical."

Lionel was a little bit shy about asking the price of her photographs. When she quoted a price, she had been paid for a photo of Bedouin children he was astounded. He had the photo of the club framed and it put behind the bar. The photo of Ali and Alice was framed and placed beside his bed. Every time Ingrid saw that photo, she loved Lionel more. She saw the photo regularly.

News came that the Bedouin who had given Alice as a present were on their way to Kano. Lionel went to see Ali and discussed whether he should give Archie to the Bedouin chief. Ali was silent for a moment and then said he would like to spend a few days in the camp so that he could introduce Archie to the other camels. Ali would also meet these other Bedouin. Lionel was pleased as Ali still regarded himself as a Bedouin and had Archie's wellbeing in mind. When he told Ingrid, she was almost in tears, Lionel and Ali were both sensitive and could almost be father and son.

Lionel and Idris went to the camp alone where they were greeted by the chief. Over the years they had met several times and there were always warm greetings but no large presents. They all understood that Alice was the ultimate present. Lionel asked whether he could bring a female photographer to the camp. They would also bring Idris's younger sister to translate for Ingrid. Lionel explained that the photographer would only take photos of anything the chief would allow. The chief asked if this lady was a friend. Lionel's reply was that he wanted to marry her in future; that even shocked Idris. The chief explained that thinking about the future was a difficult concept for Bedouin, but he would like to meet this lady.

The next day they arrived at the camp with Latifah, Idris's younger sister. Ali was following well behind with Archie. The chief welcomed them and introduced his senior wife. This was a first, and the chief asked Ingrid and Latifah to go with his wife. He then invited the men into his tent for tea and proceeded to explain that his wife wanted her photo taken. Lionel said he was surprised and the chief said he was more surprised. It was now time to spring the surprise. Lionel excused himself and said he had to go outside to call someone. Lionel summoned Ali and then he asked the chief to come outside. He then presented Archie as a gift. He explained this was the son of the camel he had been given many years ago.

The chief was visibly moved and then Lionel introduced Ali as his adopted son. Idris had some difficulty with translating "adopted". Ali would like to stay in the camp to allow Archie to meet the other camels, and as a Bedouin he wanted to be with other Bedouin. The chief put his arms around Ali and gave him a hug. Idris said he had never seen that before. Lionel explained that the only thing he required was that Ali would be treated well and returned when they moved. The chief excused himself and went to fetch his wife. He explained Ali and she hugged him and took him to the women's tent.

Later they all gathered and even the women emerged from the tent to say goodbye. There was lots of ululating and laughter, Ali was surrounded by women and he was smiling. Ingrid was ecstatic but Lionel was wondering if he had lost both Ali and Archie. Idris said that this was a day to remember he had never seen the Bedouin so relaxed, and Latifah had seen things she had to tell her parents. Many of the city dwellers had a poor opinion of the Bedouin but now she knew better.

"Sorry Lionel we have to set up a dark room. I've promised the chief's wife a photo not to be seen by any other men but her husband. I cannot tell you how magical this afternoon was, having Latifah there was a master stroke."

"Please keep your promise and not show her photo to me."

"Lionel you are such a straight fellow and I love you for the way you think. I didn't give the same promises to the other ladies and I believe at least two others are his wives. I want your opinion of my work and I'll be disappointed if you don't give me your thoughts."

The next day she set up the dark room and produced some wonderful photos. They took the photos to the camp and saw Ali playing football with other boys. Ingrid said they had to buy them a proper football.

Ingrid gave a sealed envelope to the chief, she then went to the women's tent to distribute other photos. There was another copy for the chief's wife. The chief opened the envelope and a wide grin came across his face. The chief shook hands with Lionel and Idris and kept repeating *shukran* — thanks. The next day a football was delivered to the camp.

The next month was full of pleasure and a few days before leaving Ingrid looked sad.

"Lionel I would like to come back here to live with you but I could only do that if we were married."

"I think you just proposed to me, so now I'll propose to you. I would love to marry you; you make every day a pleasure. I'm only planning to stay here a few more years and if you could stand that I would be over the moon. Where shall we get married?"

"I can set everything up in Germany and we can marry when you come on leave. Maybe you could get your parents to come to the wedding which would be in a registry office."

Lionel had not told his parents about Ingrid, now he urgently had to give them the news. He wrote to his mother and aunt and the replies were not encouraging. His mother wanted him to come home and marry an English girl. His aunt didn't seem enthusiastic and his uncle was dead against marrying a German.

Before Ingrid left Kano, Ali returned from the camp with lots of stories. Ingrid and Latifah had made a very strong positive impression on the women. Lionel was the only white man they knew and he was held in high regard. Archie was doing well and none of the other camels had attacked him, maybe they had smelled his mother and recognised he was related to the herd. Ingrid looked at Lionel after that report and asked if that could be true. Lionel couldn't be sure, but Ali had been born and brought up with camels.

"The newspapers back home will lap that up; I can't wait to tell that story. Before I leave, we do not have a photograph of both of us together. I'll set up the camera and although I don't like posed shots, I'll send you a copy so that you can send it to your parents."

"Send three copies. By the way do you have any of me alone?"

"I have regularly taken your photograph but have not developed them yet."

"I've never noticed."

"You are not supposed to notice the camera because you might start posing. I want to see you as natural as possible,"

Finally, Lionel had to ask the question: "Why did you pick me? You are an attractive lady with a profession and there must be lots of men in Germany that you could marry?"

"That first time we met in the club, I saw your face. I see many faces and I saw a kind, peaceful face. You were so helpful and kind. I saw your face when I first emerged from that dark room, your delight in seeing me, and when I emerged for the second time, I saw that same face. Dropping my towel introduced me to a new face and I liked what I saw. I think that Kano had a lot to do with my attitude to you as you have lived here many years and that told me you were a stable person. I have never seen you get angry and you do not seem to be fazed by challenging situations. You are different than any man I have met, so I decided I must have you."

"Well, you had me from the first minute we met."

Ingrid left Kano after saying goodbye to everyone, even the Emir. The photos arrived later and copies were sent to his mother and aunt. The replies to his letters were not encouraging; the photos had not changed their minds. Lionel planned his leave so that he would go to Germany to get married then take his bride to England before returning to Kano. He would fly to Bonn and Ingrid would pick him up and drive him to Leverkusen her home town, near Cologne. He had decided to stay in hotels in Coventry and Evesham as he was not sure of the reception they might receive.

Ingrid was so glad to see him she couldn't stop hugging him in the airport. The drive to her flat was filled with Ingrid talking almost non-stop. Her photographs were selling like hot cakes and her stories of the Bedouin were big news on the radio. Ingrid's flat was well-furnished and filled with photographs. Lionel realised he had been photographed many times. Ingrid cooked the dinner and it was tasty, Lionel had never tasted her cooking before, the only drawback was the wine which was too sweet for Lionel.

The next day they went to visit Ingrid's parents. Lionel was impressed with the house and her father. He owned an engineering company and spoke excellent English. Her mother was very welcoming and jokingly said that, as he had sampled Ingrid's cooking, she would prepare a real meal. The father took Lionel into the garden and asked a few questions, the answers satisfied him and then he asked Lionel if there was anything at all wrong with Ingrid. Lionel replied her taste in wine. Her father descended into fits of laughter.

"Your daughter came to Kano and fitted into the environment immediately, her photographs have made me look at things around me that never made an impression on me previously. Your daughter knows what she wants and goes for it."

"That is very true, from an early age we saw an independent streak. At school she was a bit of a rebel but always near the top in the highest class. She loved English and we were living in the British zone, so she had plenty of practice. Photography came from an uncle who gave her the first camera. In this area her photographs and talks on radio are well received. Your name is well known in this area. By the way, let me donate a few French wines to your cause, I also have a couple of Australian wines you might appreciate."

"In the club we have Greek and Italian wine and occasionally French wine, but I have never tried Australian wine."

The dinner was very good with too much food on the table and a couple of good bottles of wine. Lionel was invited to visit the father's factory during the following afternoon; it was assumed he would like a lie-in after all that food. Ingrid was looking forward to a long lie-in.

Lionel's family would not come to the wedding and the event was low-key. Some of Ingrid's family came and the reception was in a local restaurant. Lionel apologised to Ingrid's father that he knew little or no German but he was sure Ingrid would give him a translation. Ingrid's father gave half of his speech in German and half in English. Lionel apologised that his speech would be in English unless they preferred Arabic or Hausa. He thought that his joke had fallen flat until there was an eruption of laughter. There was a band after the dinner and of course Lionel had to dance. Luckily, he remembered a basic waltz he had learned at school. Ingrid said she would have to teach him to jive.

They spent the next few days in Germany and then set off to England. Ingrid had visited London but had never ventured north. They had a hotel in the centre of Coventry and had to visit the cathedral. Lionel was a little apprehensive about that visit but Ingrid was too engrossed in taking photos. The visit to his parents started off tense until his father and Ingrid got into a discussion of the cost of living. His mother was quiet until Ingrid showed her some photos of Lionel. His mother admitted to Lionel that Ingrid must love him.

The visit to Evesham was a little less tense. Ingrid loved Evesham and Lionel's aunt was very welcoming. When his uncle asked Ingrid where she learnt English. She explained she had lived in the British Zone of Germany and had plenty of contact with British soldiers and officers. After that his uncle softened and a few photos of camels and Lionel had him interested in Nigeria.

Ingrid had to visit Stratford and Lionel became second to the camera, except at night. She was delighted at the countryside around Evesham and told Lionel that they had return someday so she could see more. She was disappointed that they couldn't see a play at the theatre in Stratford, as all the plays were booked out.

The journey back to Kano was interrupted by a short stay in Cairo; again, Lionel was a long way second to the camera. Their arrival in Kano was a time for celebration. Ali hugged Ingrid and said he could call her mother. Ingrid had to suppress tears and told Lionel that was a present she had not expected; it was the best present. Idris, Ahmed and Latifah were invited to the club for small reception.

Latifah was disappointed that Ingrid didn't bring her wedding dress to Kano. Ahmed and Idris were interested in England and were surprised that the couple didn't visit London. Lionel explained that there was a lot more to England than London.

A Frenchman showed up with a couple of good French wines but there were no Germans in town. Lionel was starting to enjoy wine.

The next few years passed very peacefully and Ingrid spent a lot of time at the camel farm. Ali was teaching her Arabic and she was helping him with English. She had taken motherhood to heart and Lionel was very impressed. Ingrid was also showing Ali what she did with the camera. Some Bedouin groups came and Ali visited them all. He found that some of the groups, particularly those from the west were not so friendly and he warned Lionel. The Emir was a little bit worried with rumbles from the south, he had been told of some Ibos leaving to go south. He asked Lionel if he would visit some of the surrounding states and talk to the Emirs. He wanted an independent opinion of the changes.

Ingrid was very happy to see more of northern Nigeria but Lionel warned that some of the Emirs might be more conservative than his friend.

"I'll hide behind my husband and peak out to get a photograph."

"Ingrid I'm being serious."

"I'm only joking. Can we take Ali?"

"That might be a good idea we could let him see more than Kano and he could talk about camels if anyone was interested. He will meet people we might not get to see. First stop will be Kaduna and you should have a stock of those pills you take."

"Lionel those are contraceptives and I was thinking of giving them up as they give me headaches. If I give them up, we might have a child. Now do I take them or not?"

"I'll take my chance but let me know as soon as you can because I'll have to make arrangements. Your headaches might change to a very special headache."

"I think you have let me know your opinion but you'll be the first to know."

They both laughed and then planned their trip.

Visits to the surrounding states resulted in overtime for Ingrid's camera. Ali was very excited at all the towns they visited and he met a few Bedouin groups. His news was that there were many problems in the east and the west and the groups were not going deep into Egypt and were cautious about Algeria. Ali had no idea where these countries were but he wanted to tell his father, Lionel.

The news for the Emir was that most states were operating normally but the army was actively recruiting. Many Ibos had left and gone south. The Emir sent an emissary to Lagos to find out what was happening. The emissary returned to say that a Colonel Ojukwu had declared that the state of Biafra would secede from Nigeria. Lionel had news for the Emir, Ingrid was pregnant and he would have to resign and take her to Germany. The Emir said he understood but that he didn't expect the war would get this far north.

Ingrid told Ali the news that she and Lionel would go to live in Germany as she was having a baby and wanted to be near a good hospital.

"Yes, you must go so that my brother will be born in the best hospital."

"It could be a girl; you could have a sister."

"I would like a brother but if a sister comes, I'll be happy, it's your choice."

When she told Lionel of this conversation, she said she was not sure how she stopped bursting into tears. Lionel realised that he needed to formally adopt Ali and so started the proceedings. The Emir said Ali would continue at school and they would look after him. When he was older, he could visit Germany and possibly live there. Lionel told Ali he would write to him and send photos of the baby. In a year or two Lionel would visit Kano to see him. Ali was calm and said it was all in the hands of Allah. Lionel couldn't but admire Ali's attitude.

There was a big party at the airport as Ingrid and Lionel left Nigeria. In the south the war was going on and they had to fly directly to Cairo. All the way Lionel was thinking what he was going to do now. Ingrid had privately, and unknown to Lionel, told her father, Ernst, to give him a job. That was not hard as her father liked Lionel.

Ingrid's flat in Germany was two bedrooms and one could be converted to a nursery. Ernst wanted them to sell the flat and buy a house; he would help with the finances. Lionel explained that he would like that but that he didn't have a job. Ernst said he had a job with his company and now they had to work out what he could do. Lionel explained he was really a bookkeeper and could he look at the books?

"Of course you can, they belong to Ingrid when I die and if they belong to Ingrid they belong to you."

Lionel visited the factory, went through the books and found that most of the products were used in Germany, with little export. Lionel put together a list of products with photos, of course, to take to England; Coventry and Birmingham were his destinations.

He was not keen to take Ingrid with him as she was well into her pregnancy but she would not stay at home.

"Lionel you are too protective and I want to see your parents and Evesham."

Lionel was not too sure about meeting his parents but he hoped the pregnancy would change their opinions. He was surprised by their welcome, a grandchild had reversed attitudes. Lionel still didn't tell them about Ali; that would have to wait till later. Lionel visited several companies and there was some enthusiasm for his wares. He investigated all the customs and excise regulations and came to the conclusion that he should set up an export/import company in England. All he needed initially was a post box and to register a company. He would discuss the details with Ernst when he got back to Leverkusan.

The baby was born and it was a boy. Lionel wanted to name him Archie but Ingrid wanted to know what Ali would say, she was really missing him. Ali's reply was a surprise; his suggestion was Biyulionel basically meaning Number Two Lionel. Ingrid couldn't stop crying when she read the letter.

"This boy tears at my heart strings, he has to come to live with us. Ali wanted to call him after you — that is a real son. Archie is going to be a second name; I don't care if no one understands the first name. We and Ali understand and that is all that is important."

Trade with England was going well and Ernst found a house in the area for Lionel to buy. Now they could invite Ali to come to Germany. Finally, Lionel informed his family of Ali and said they would visit England when Ali had adjusted to Germany.

Lionel took Ali to England and Ali's stories about camels had them all spell-bound and then he told them about Lionel's time in Kano and he had the family in the palm of his hands. Ali gave a talk about camels on the local radio and Lionel's relatives could talk about nothing else. Ali soon learned German but decided to go to university in England.

Ingrid was so proud of Ali, and Biyulionel loved his brother. Ali was a good brother and loved to play with his little brother and help him with school projects. Stories about the desert had Biyulionel telling his mother he had to go see for himself when he was older. Ingrid's photographs were okay but he wanted to smell the desert. Ingrid was thinking she never smelled the desert and when she took photos in future, she had to smell what she was photographing. Ali again was teaching her something new.

Ali was going to university and was discussing his choice with Lionel.

"Father, I want to study economics, is that okay?"
"You can study whatever you want, we'll be pleased whatever you do and I'm sure you'll get camels in there somewhere."

"I'll also try to get the Bedouin in there somewhere."

They both laughed and Lionel was thinking what a wonderful son. He has to take over the company I have inherited.

As Lionel came towards retirement, he would have more time to spend with Ingrid. Early retirement allowed him to look back at his life and realise his good fortune. He had two sons, one at university and the other graduated with a good profession. Ali was taking over, and Biyulionel would fit into the family business. Nigeria had made Lionel a man. He controlled a large company, his wife was a renowned photographer and his two sons were totally capable of replacing him.

He marvelled that he was just a simple bookkeeper.

The Coward

"Are you a coward? Are you going to let them beat you? I don't care, I have given up on you — go home, you're too old to try anymore."

These last words stirred Dave into action; he threw over the table, breaking the glasses and splashing beer all over the terrazzo floor.

"Why do you want to fight me and not them?" Dave was confronted by his young friend Arthur, his new adversary. "Is there any satisfaction in hitting me? Fight them." That phrase, "fight them" was constantly buzzing around in Dave's head. "I don't want to fight you or them I just want to get out and go home."

The waiter walked towards the pair and in his best English asked them to leave the bar. "You must go, leave now!" They both left without protest and Arthur left a tip on the table for the waiter. "I've been thrown out of some places but the airport hotel bar must be the lowest." Arthur's jibe made no impression upon Dave who opened the door vigorously and stepped out into the hot, humid Lagos air. Arthur followed and walked a couple of paces behind. They walked to the car park ignoring the calls of the "night eagles", ignoring everything, but especially each other. They were old friends yet new enemies.

Dave was a big man, a muscular ex-marine, past his prime at forty-five but still a force to be reckoned with. His hair was short with no bald spots and he was slim with no hint of a boozer's belly although he could consume a large amount of beer. The muscles in his arms indicated his physical strength and when he wore shorts, his muscular legs confirmed the complete man. He was bronzed by the sun and Nigeria was the perfect place to show off his physique. His problem was that he was used to a disciplined life and this place was chaos. The paradise he had expected turned out to be hell. One step before the next didn't work here, and there seemed to be no logical movement in anything that happened. Work was a disaster; he would get things moving in a positive direction only to find a little later that it was all going wrong. When he was around the workers, they were sullen and quiet and as he was leaving, he would hear the laughing and joking. He couldn't understand Yoruba but he could understand the tone in their voices. "You have to have eyes in your backside, no discipline, no sense of direction." These were Dave's new catch phrases, but Arthur seemed to see more. That bothered Dave because Arthur was like a son, and he was young and foolish. Dave had seen the world and Arthur had never been to Scotland, Ireland or Wales and Wales was so close to Manchester. Arthur had been abroad, on holiday for two weeks in the Costa del Sol. When Dave first learnt this, he had laughed and called it the fish-and-chip capital of Spain. Thoughts of Korea, Malaya and Aden were still fresh in Dave's mind; the army had taken him to many other places but the different cultures in those three places had struck him the most. The problem was that Arthur was handling this horrendous place much better, the explosion was inevitable.

Where Dave was large Arthur was small, five feet four with a belly as big as a confirmed middle-aged drinker. He never exercised and Dave had never seen him run. He had a sallow complexion and long hair, he could be taken for a hippie. He was good with figures and books and that had bought him to Nigeria to be the company accountant. Nigeria had also been a shock to Arthur but he realised he must be flexible in thought, word and deed; it was going to be the key to survival in this difficult place. Although he was an accountant and loved order and discipline his physical stature had always dictated diplomacy, except now. Dave was both a father figure and a protector and as a team they could manage this place, but Dave was cracking up. For once Arthur had thrown caution to the wind and had challenged Dave because Dave wanted to leave Nigeria. The consequences could have been disastrous but the chance was worth taking, Arthur couldn't let his friend fold under pressure. He wanted to talk at length to Dave on the subject but the upturned table had put that idea on hold.

They had met a couple of years earlier when they had both been recruited to work in a factory near the airport. As the only two English employees they were in constant contact and formed a friendship. They lived together, ate together and slept in the same house. Their accommodation was not luxurious but adequate.

Both men were silent as they walked to reach the company car. Arthur climbed into the front seat next to the driver and Dave sprawled in the back. They were silent as they were transported to the Guest House. Tomorrow they were going to Ibadan and the journey was on both their minds. The driver smiled weakly at both men as they alighted from the car but got no recognition in return, he suspected there was a problem but was afraid to ask.

"Seven thirty in the morning — don't be late," barked Dave as they entered the house. Arthur gave Dave a weak smile but only got an icy stare in return, so they both retired to their separate bedrooms.

Breakfast was held in silence and the silence in the car was almost unbearable as they raced along the Ibadan expressway. The road was a new four-lane highway and if there was a speed limit no one seemed to notice or care. One problem was trucks which seemed to occupy both lanes at one time. This morning the road was fairly clear as most of the traffic was going the other way towards Lagos. They were making good time when suddenly the car started to lurch from side to side finally rolling over several times and landing on the passenger side. They had ploughed off the road into the bush — semi-jungle. Part of the road had subsided and the tarmac had become rippled and curved, they had hit this at high speed and the frantic moving of the steering wheel by the driver had caused the car to roll.

Dave was first to stir, he had been thrown about in the backseat as he had no seat belt. The car was on its side and Dave had to kick open one of the back doors. As he crawled out, he realised his left arm was useless and the whole of his left side was in excruciating pain. He lay on the grass for a few moments and then realised Arthur was still in the car. He had to get Arthur out before the car caught fire. He hobbled over to the car, his left ankle was also a problem. He wrenched open the driver's door and with one hand lifted the driver bodily from the tangled wreck. He threw the driver to the ground, he had not been wearing a seat belt but Arthur was. Arthur was unconscious and Dave realised the only way to get him out was to put the car back on four wheels.

Dave frantically pulled and pushed the car, to no avail. Tears were streaming down his face; it was not pain it was the realisation that his little friend might be dead or about to die in a fire ball. He must get some leverage on the car, so he went to a nearby tree and tore a large branch from the tree. With the aid of a large stone and a few hefty tugs on the branch he was able to get the car on four wheels. In the meantime, the driver had awoken to watch in amazement the physical power Dave had unleashed. Dave had not noticed the driver as all his energies had been devoted to rescuing Arthur.

The passenger door was mangled and it took all Dave's strength to tear it open. He unbuckled the unconscious Arthur and felt his pulse. Arthur was alive and Dave carefully lifted him and placed him gently on the ground well away from the car. That was the last Dave remembered.

"Back in the land of the living, I thought I would have to spend another day sitting by this bed." Arthur's voice seemed distant but Dave caught every word, he opened his eyes to see Arthur leaning over him.

"Get me a drink of water, my throat feels like a dry mud hole — better still, get me a whisky. I ache all over. How long have I been here and where is here?"

This is a private hospital in Ibadan and you have been here four days."

"Four days!"

"Yes, four days, you've broken your left arm and four ribs. Your left leg is badly bruised but not broken and you have big splinters in your right hand," Arthur said with a chuckle. "After you rescued me, you passed out and have only been semi-conscious a few times." Arthur relayed these facts as matter-of-factly as if he were reading a financial statement, but then added in an excited tone, "You are a hero."

"Water first and "Why?" second, and did the car catch fire?"

As Dave slowly sipped his water Arthur proceeded to tell him all the news:

"The driver saw you take the car apart with one hand to rescue me. He does nothing all day but tell the story and every time he tells it gets more incredible. The workers at the factory have lapped it up and they are working like demons for you. All you told them in the past that they either forgot or ignored is now being done. The manager is strutting around the factory saying your name with a big grin. The workers have had one big party and when I let them know you are awake, they will have a bigger one. The story is all over Ibadan as well. The truck driver who bought us to Ibadan stopped as you were getting the driver out. He watched at a safe distance while this mad white man took apart a car, he thought you had gone berserk. He has been telling the story all over town. We were very lucky the car didn't go up in flames or I would not be telling you this news."

Dave tried to sit up but his chest gave him such a sharp pain that it was futile. "Don't try to move — you only have strapping around your chest. They have set your arm but may have to break it when we get back to England. Tomorrow I'm going to try to do all the formalities, we'll both fly out as soon as I can arrange transport. A coincidence, we came in on the same plane and are flying out on the same plane." Arthur was trying to make light of the problem.

"All the workers hope you'll come back for the biggest party."

"What about you? I wasn't sure whether you were dead until I got that stupid car on its wheels."

"I was just unconscious I think I was so scared, my brain switched off," Arthur said jokingly. "I've had a couple of headaches and got a few bruises but I'm glad I was wearing the seat belt."

"That bloody seat belt was the reason I had to go to all that trouble. Next time I sit in the front. Am I a coward, indeed? I'm coming back as soon as I can. I'll get that factory working as never before."

Apapa Docks

Apapa was the main dock area of Lagos, although there was a dock at Lagos Port. The whole area was surrounded by industry, much of it not far advanced from crude. When I knew it, the area was a nightmare to drive to or through. That was not the case when Mario first jumped ship in the 1950s. Mario was from Sicily and not long after the war had signed on as a deck hand on a cargo ship. He had been to South America, the US and even Australia but found that jumping ship in organised countries was difficult. He hated the ship he was on and when he was told they were going to trade along the West African coast, he thought he might try his luck again. After stopping at a few ports along the coast he decided that Apapa was the place to try his luck. Once ashore he had no idea where to go but found a shop run by a Greek and asked if he could get a job. The old Greek merchant understood that Mario had jumped ship and gave him a place to stay until the ship left port.

Mario was a good temporary lodger and he was very happy to help with the cooking, housework and serving in the shop. The owner said he couldn't pay him but would try to find him a job. A couple of his customers who used the shop regularly were an English man and his wife who had an export/import business. They needed help with the ever-increasing volume of items coming through the port. The British civil servants who were running the administration were aware that independence was coming and any European with a passport who wanted to work and to live in Nigeria had a very easy passage to get a work permit. The English couple, John and Anne, were in a very good position, they were dealing with the British administrators and the rich families in Lagos. They also knew that come independence they would need a Nigerian partner, preferably a silent partner; they also needed a young man to take some of the load off John.

Just after the war John had been in the army and was stationed in Lagos. He had married Anne and bought her to live in Lagos for a year. She loved it and so when he retired from the army they stayed and opened a business. John was an easy going fellow and was liked by the local Nigerians and those in the army; this was to become useful after independence. He also found that the richer Nigerians wanted lots of goods from the UK, such as washing machines and cookers. Many wealthy Nigerians had lived in the UK and saw the benefits of such items. One item that was in high demand was toilets and the plumbing that went with such an item. John hooked up with a manufacturer in the UK who supplied the toilet bowls and fittings, with suitable instructions for installation. Toilets became one of his biggest imports, after a slow start.

John and Anne rented a house from a Nigerian called Johnathon who lived in Ibadan. Johnathon was originally from Lagos but had moved to Ibadan after his father's death, His father had built the house but Johnathon couldn't live in the house where his father had died, so had moved the family north. Johnathon had a trucking company which operated between Ibadan and Lagos and John and Anne were his customers and he theirs. Johnathon had been approached by the couple to be a partner in their business, he was very happy but he wanted to carry on his trucking business and wanted to have no real input into the export/import side of the deal. Just the partnership John and Anne desired.

Mario started work with the couple and soon picked up on the way things worked. He was learning English rapidly and was having lots of contact with Johnathon. They often joked that English was their second language, that and their age, their friendly disposition made them soul mates. Mario had a room in John and Anne's house and often treated them to a Sicilian meal. Towards independence in 1960 the work load in shipping seemed to be expanding exponentially. Mario was busy all the time but he could still get an occasional visit to Ibadan where he was treated like a king. Mario was earning good money and decided he needed a wife. He contacted his family in Sicily and asked that they find him a wife. John and Anne were amused but didn't let their feelings be known, Johnathon, however, understood completely — any wife should have the approval of the family.

Mario went off to Sicily to marry a lady called Alicia (not exactly a common Sicilian name) Mario explained that in Sicily there were many seafaring families that had settled from all over the Mediterranean. John and Anne soon realised that Mario had been carrying a heavy load and they were longing for him to return. Mario returned after two weeks with his very pretty new wife, who spoke some English. John and Anne were very welcoming and suggested that Mario might rent another house and they would pay the rent. Mario replied that if it was okay with them, they would stay as they were; the space in this house was greater than anything they would have in Sicily.

Mario took his new bride to Ibadan to the biggest party Alicia had ever attended. There was a band, drummers welcoming them, food and drinks galore. Johnathon had a sister called Honesty and she and Alicia hit it off immediately and talked for a long time. Johnathon remarked to Mario that his sister had not talked to anyone for so long, she was missing Lagos and had almost become a recluse in Ibadan. Mario said that John's house was full, but if they could find her a flat in Apapa they would look after her. Johnathon was worried about sending his sister to Lagos but Mario's suggestion was a great idea. Johnathon admired Mario who could simplify a complex situation and make it easy; he did that in business as well.

Independence was now in full swing but the only effect for John and Mario was that there was more work. Anne was taking a back seat and spending more time with the ladies. They made an odd trio when they went shopping in Lagos Island. Honesty's Yoruba, Anne's English and Alicia's haggling skills made them a formidable force.

One day the ladies were at home when a young policeman came to talk to Mario. Mario was not in the office so this policeman had come to his home. They invited him in for tea and had a good chat. He had been in England and had spent some time in Birmingham, attached to the local force. He was handsome, well-spoken and with a good sense of humour. The three women were captivated. Anne asked the probing questions, where was he from? He was from Lagos State having been born in Yaba. What of his family? Where did they live? His father was a trader and now lived on Victoria Island. It was funny but here was a policeman being interrogated. He took it all in good spirits and was enjoying his time until Mario arrived.

Mario and Ayo adjourned to another room and the ladies giggled about this handsome new stranger. Ayo was visiting Mario to discuss a problem of drug importation. The police were worried about illegal drugs passing through Apapa docks. Mario was asked to let the police know if there were any suspicious imports and to clear them. The police would see to the rest. Mario said that that day a man, he had not seen before had come to his office to clear some special cement to make roofing tiles. Mario had thought this strange but had found the paperwork in order and had cleared about twenty bags. They were to be picked up tomorrow. The strange thing was, that cement generally came in by the ship load and twenty bags meant this must be special stuff. Ayo thanked him, wished the ladies goodbye and left. Mario was a bit bemused by the demeanour of the ladies but thought nothing more of it.

Ayo was a regular visitor and was not upset when Mario was not present. The police had caught several shipments of illegal drugs and he wanted Mario to relax so that suspicion didn't fall on him. Mario knew most of the items cleared in Apapa and he could pinpoint other items cleared by other agents, he seemed to have a nose for it and he was glad to get this "rubbish" off the streets. Honesty and Ayo were starting to become interested in each other so Mario invited Johnathon to meet Ayo. As Johnathon travelled to Lagos, he had only positive thoughts about Mario; here he was invited to meet his sister's suitor, just as would happen in the family — Mario was family.

Johnathon found his sister livelier than he had known her for years and a young policeman who impressed him. After talking to him for a few minutes Johnathon realised that Ayo would make a good brother-in-law. The whole gathering sat down to an

Italian feast provided by Alicia and Italian wine provided by Mario. John and Anne realised this was a good time to retire and go back to England. They had made enough money and wanted time to enjoy it. John took Johnathon aside and asked if he would take Mario on as a partner when they retired. Johnathon had no hesitation in saying yes, in fact he had thought of a partnership for a long time. They made the announcement at the party and then there was another announcement, the engagement of Ayo and Honesty.

Johnathon was in his element, he had three parties to give: one for the engagement, one for the partnership with Mario and one for John and Anne leaving. He wanted three separate parties: the engagement celebration would be in Ibadan, the partnership party would be in Apapa, and the departure of John and Anne in Lagos. The first one was in Ibadan and all Ayo's relatives had to be invited. This was a huge party that filled all the local hotels, Mario, Alicia, John and Anne stayed in Johnathon's house. This party went for three days and when Mario and the others left, it was still in progress. The partnership party in Apapa was a little more subdued with lots of people from Apapa invited and also the Italian Ambassador. The third party was at the Victoria Hotel where the guest list included the British High Commissioner and several of his staff including the consul. There were many of the rich Lagotian families and anyone Mario could identify as old customers. This was a more formal affair but a good party nevertheless.

When John and Anne finally departed Lagos there were many tears. Honesty said their honeymoon would be in England, and Mario said he would bring Alicia to England as she had seen nothing but Italy and Nigeria; Johnathon said he would buy a flat in London and visit when he could get away. All the promises were kept and John had a great time introducing his friends at the local pub.

Ayo was rising in the ranks and Honesty was enjoying being a married woman. Mario and Johnathon were going gang busters and Lagos Airport had become a freight hub so they opened an office near the airport. Alicia went to Italy for one month a year but she enjoyed the other time in Apapa; she had gathered a group of expatriate ladies and they had meeting at the house and Honesty was often present. Apapa was becoming a rougher area and Mario had a wall built around the house, he also employed a day guard and a night guard. Mario had to take on a young deputy and the airport office was managed by a cousin of Johnathon.

Mario spent a lot of time in the airport office and the Ikeja Club was his relaxation place. He said he felt more at ease in Ikeja where fewer people knew him, and he was less bothered by customers. As the two offices began to run smoothly Mario started to take Sundays off so he could do the books and relax. He often took Alicia to the Ikeja Club which is where Arthur met him. Arthur was the membership secretary of the club and one of the older members introduced him to Mario. Arthur's wife and Alicia hit it off and they chatted for most of the afternoon. Arthur would see Mario and Alicia about two Sundays in the month and his wife was invited to one of Alicia's gatherings.

They drove down to Apapa one Tuesday afternoon and almost got lost. After arriving Alicia said Arthur should go to see Mario at the office which gladly was in walking distance. He passed several textile factories all spewing coloured water into the open sewers before he reached the office. When he arrived, he asked Mario where the factories were getting the water as most parts of Lagos had water shortages. The main drinking water plant had been built in the twenties and couldn't cope with the demand. Mario said they all had bore holes and this was causing a problem with land sinkage occurring in the area. His house was a few feet above the surrounding area but expected that one day, it too, might start to sink.

Mario took Arthur to the docks and he had never seen so many containers and other large objects distributed in such a haphazard manner. Arthur asked how they found anything and Mario's reply was that if they could catch it as it was unloaded from the boat, they would get it to their office; if not, Mario's deputy would spend many hours searching for it.

Arthur was going on leave to the UK and his wife wanted to bring some things back as three growing children needed clothes and toys not readily available in Nigeria. Mario said, "Get me the paperwork and when you return bring me the keys to the trunk, and make sure you specify Apapa docks."

Arthur went on leave and took a trunk to Liverpool and had it put on a ship unloading at Apapa docks. He sent the paperwork through the airport office and decided to drop the keys off in Apapa. His children were in the University of Lagos School and he was to drop them off and make his way to Apapa. He set off early in the morning as it was raining and knew the traffic would be difficult, but it was impossible. After one hour they were not close to the university, so he decide to go to Apapa, that was also impossible as there were road closures and so he had to turn back home arriving near midday. Arthur phoned Mario and explained the problem. Mario understood and said he would get the trunk cleared when he could get transport. Mario would let him know, by getting in touch with the club. That could be a while as truck traffic was stuck due to flooding in the Apapa area. That was the last Arthur heard from Mario — he was dead a few weeks after their phone conversation. Arthur received his trunk and not long after a rumour went around that Mario had been murdered.

One Sunday, as was his practice Mario was at home 'doing the books' and his deputy was in the office. The day watchman had wanted to go to a wake and so Mario had let him go. The night watchman would come on duty at about 5 p.m. Alicia was visiting Italy for her annual month and so Mario was alone. When the night watchman came at 5 pm. he noticed the front metal gate ajar instead of being locked. He went to the front door which was locked and banged on it to get his master. There was no answer so he went around the back and found the door shut but unlocked. He entered the kitchen shouting all the time for his master, with no reply he went to the living room where he found Mario lying in a pool of blood, his throat had been cut. The watchman then ran straight to the police station. Luckily the local chief of police was there and he immediately phoned the Lagos State chief of police.

Ayo answered the phone and couldn't believe what he was hearing. He ordered that no one enter the house and the area to be sealed off, he would be there as soon as possible. He also ordered that they call the forensic police and that they should meet him there. Ayo was so glad Honesty was not at home — she was at a wake in Ibadan. He guessed that Johnathon and Segun, the airport office manager, would also be there.

When Ayo reached the house, he realised that no one had checked if Mario was actually dead. He escorted the forensic team into the house and warned them not to touch anything and to tread carefully. He knew the procedures as he had carried them out in the UK but was worried one of the team might forget the protocols. Mario was dead and Ayo was able to identify the victim. The safe was open and the keys were in

Mario's hand. They photographed everything and Ayo checked that the front door was locked. He could see no evidence of a struggle and Mario's throat had been deeply cut. Ayo asked the doctor how long Mario had been dead and the doctor said he couldn't tell for sure but by the state and pattern of the blood it must have been several hours.

In the kitchen there was a pot of cold coffee and two cups. Otherwise, there was nothing out of the ordinary, but Ayo took a good look as he had spent many hours in that kitchen. Ayo left for his office and ordered that he wanted a preliminary report on his desk later that evening and commanded that when the team left the house it was to be sealed and several policemen left to guard the house. Arriving at his office he now had a few dreaded phone calls to make. He was not sure where the wake was taking place but he had to let Johnathon and Honesty know the bad news. He had no phone number in Italy to let Alicia know but he would tell the Italian Ambassador. He sat at his desk pondering the scene and what could have happened. Mario obviously knew his killer, they had drunk coffee together, probably after breakfast. Mario had opened the safe. Had he been forced to do so or was he going to get something from the safe? There had been no struggle suggesting the assailant had come from behind. Ayo had never seen that safe open and didn't know what it contained. He was feeling weary but had to wait for the report.

The report arrived later that evening and it was short and to the point. Death had probably been almost instantaneous the cut was very deep indicating a strong killer. The time of death was difficult to pinpoint but may have been at about 10 a.m. There were no fingerprints on the safe which contained no money only invoices and accounts. There were no fingerprints on the cups, saucers or the coffee pot. The fingerprints on the back door handle were only those of the night watchman. Everything so far examined indicated that the fingerprints had been wiped clean suggesting the killer was not in too much of a hurry. Ayo was sitting pondering the report when the phone rang, it was Johnathon. He sounded very upset and said Honesty had not stopped crying. They would set out for Lagos tomorrow morning, it was not safe to drive at night.

The next morning Ayo went to Apapa to see the forensic police and talk to the Apapa commander. The local police were interviewing almost everyone in the area as well as the two guards. They had contacted Mario's deputy and an officer was on his way to question him. Ayo was agitated and said vehemently that this case had to be solved by the Lagos police. Back in his office he was formulating another plan of attack. He called into his office a young officer who had recently returned from a training trip in the UK. This officer, Eugene, was not from Lagos, he was an Ibo who had been brought to Lagos as a young boy after the Biafra war. Ayo instructed him to look at all the reports coming in to the office and decide on his own plan of action. When Eugene came to Ayo's office, he should be in uniform but at other times could be in plain clothes. He was to try to identify suspects and do background checks and be as discrete as possible and not let the Apapa police know of his interest in the case.

Not long after Eugene had left the office Johnathon, Honesty and Segun arrived. They were all shaken by the events and this was a very sombre meeting, Honesty was in tears and the other two not far off but Ayo had to ask a few questions. Had they ever seen the safe open and did they know what it contained? None of them had ever seen the safe open but Segun knew that there would be money, account books and invoices. Mario had often said that when he got back home, he would check the books in the safe. Any money taken on Friday afternoon or Saturday would not have been banked. Segun pointed out that as he was in Ibadan on Friday and Saturday, the money taken at the airport office would still be in his safe. Ayo thought money in the safe would only be from the Apapa office. Who had been to the office on Friday and Saturday?

Ayo sent Honesty home and went with Johnathon and Segun to Apapa. He made them wear gloves and asked them to look at the books and invoices from the safe. There was also one book on a table in the living room. This book was immediately identified as containing the latest transactions. Segun identified items from the airport and those from the dock. Most of the books and invoices in the safe were old and he thought there must be some newer ones in the other office.

Ayo instructed the Apapa police chief to take Mario's deputy (also called Ayo) in for further questioning while he would take Johnathon and Segun to have a look at the office. Ayo, the deputy, was to be asked about all the visitors in the week and whether he thought Mario would have seen them all or left some to the deputy Ayo. He was to be asked whether any items had been recently cleared and any items long on the dock uncleared. The instruction was to keep him away from the office for at least two hours. Ayo the deputy was to be asked if Mario had refused to clear any items. Ayo was now starting to think about the early interactions with Mario that had resulted in drug convictions. Drugs were still coming into Lagos but recently there had been a lull in drug busts. Any clients who only dealt with Ayo the deputy might be suspects so there was a need to know who they were.

Ayo, Johnathon and Segun entered the dock office and looked through the filing cabinets. There was a safe but neither Johnathon nor Segun had a key. Ayo had thought of this and had duplicates made of any key (in Mario's hand) that didn't fit the house safe. The office safe contained a small amount of money and two recent transaction books. There were several outstanding items not yet cleared and a good number awaiting collection. Ayo noted those uncleared in Ayo the deputy's name, he would have them searched when he had a warrant. They found nothing untoward in the office and they were gone in an hour.

Back at his office Ayo realised that only Alicia might know what was in the safe and she would be back in a day or so. The Italian police and Scotland Yard had offered help but he wanted this case solved by his own men; this was personal. Eugene entered the office and said that the only person without a corroborated alibi was Mario's deputy and that he was trying to find out more about him. Ayo confided in Eugene that there may be a drug connection and gave him a list of the customers he had noted from the book in the office. These people were to be investigated quietly as he suspected drug smuggling was being aided by someone in the police force. Nothing new came out of the interview with the deputy except that Mario would often see clients in the morning and in the afternoon go to the airport. This was confirmed by Segun. Ayo asked Segun if Mario had turned down any customers at the airport and Segun told him there were quite a few and he could name some of them. These now went into a new list for Eugene to investigate.

Ayo was thinking that Eugene's list was getting too big but who else could he trust? The Italian Ambassador was on the phone and was asking when the body might be released for burial. He had spoken to the priest at the Sacred Heart Church and he wanted to wait for Alicia. Ayo assured him that the body was being treated well and they would do whatever Alicia asked. The press were now onto the case — it could hardly be kept secret. Ayo was not yet ready to give any interviews. The state governor had not yet contacted him but he was expecting that shortly, as the whole diplomatic community was abuzz.

Alicia arrived, Ayo, Honesty, Johnathon and the Italian Ambassador met her at the airport. Ayo wanted to be delicate but he had to ask her a few questions in private. They all went back to Ayo's house and Ayo asked if Alicia wanted to go to the house. Luckily, she said yes and that was the opportunity to get her alone. After lunch they were driven to Apapa and Ayo apologised for asking questions, but she understood. She would do anything to catch the killer of the love of her life. First, he asked about the safe. She had seen the safe open many times and she knew where the key was kept. In the safe he kept money, books and lots of personal items. Mario treasured a few of the gifts he had been given and he would even take them out on occasions to remember old times; Mario was very sentimental. Most of the items were not valuable: things such as key rings, badges and pins, they all had a story. His prized possession was a medal presented to him by the Italian Ambassador for service to Italy and a gold cigarette case presented by John and Anne when they left. There was also, funnily enough, a cigarette ash tray with the inscription, *To Mario for services rendered.*

Mario didn't smoke. That last item alerted Ayo as an ash tray had been found in the garden.

Alicia was very calm when she entered the house and was very willing to wear gloves. They first entered the kitchen and Ayo asked if she saw anything out of the ordinary as it was left as it had been found. Yes, Mario was using the best china; on his own he would have a mug of coffee. The breakfast things had been washed up which meant he had had time to do the washing and drying. The cutlery draw was open, not like Mario who would never leave a drawer open. When they reached the living room the body had been removed and the blood cleaned but everything else was in its place. Alicia said that anyone Mario knew or who was invited would be let in through the front door and Mario would lock it after the guest entered. So the back door was an escape route thought Ayo. Alicia asked if she could go upstairs and Ayo said certainly. She entered their bedroom and could see nothing amiss but when she entered the bathroom and saw Mario's dressing gown she broke down. Ayo tried to console her, but in a few minutes, she pulled herself together and calmly told Ayo she couldn't live in this house again.

As soon as he reached the office Ayo called the forensic police. Had they fingerprinted the ash tray? Had they found other things like medals or key rings in the garden? They had not fingerprinted anything from the garden, so he told them to do it immediately. The only two items the killer might not throw away were the

Italian medal and the cigarette case. Ayo went home to a very sad and sombre household. Johnathon was talking about selling the house where his father and his "second father" had died. Honesty was consoling Alicia but it appeared Honesty needed the most consoling.

The next day Eugene informed Ayo that he had followed Ayo the deputy to a house near where he lived. He had emerged a few hours later seemingly a bit disturbed. Eugene wanted to enquire about the house with the local police but decided that might alert someone so he was asking if Ayo could make discrete enquiries. Ayo had picked the right man. Eugene also informed Ayo that a couple of the customers on Ayo's list were a bit shady. Ayo had Segun's list but he would not overload Eugene so he would find someone in the Ikeja police to investigate these characters.

The next day the forensic police said they had a partial print on the underside of the ashtray but there were no prints on the other small items. Ayo called in the local Lagos Island commander and asked about the house — who owned it and its use. The commander sheepishly said that they suspected it was a gambling house. Ayo's retort was that the owner should be escorted to Ayo's office within the hour. Ayo then contacted the Apapa Port Authority and asked for a list of authorised clearing agents. He was not done yet, he wanted all suspected drug cases from the whole of Lagos State; an order which sent his office into overdrive.

The gambling-house owner was ushered into Ayo's office and everyone asked to leave. The man was a bit confused but here there was no protection (if he had any) and he was not sure what he would be asked. Ayo came right to the point, they knew he kept an illegal gaming house but that was not on the agenda, unless he would not cooperate. Ayo asked what he knew about Ayo the deputy who had been visiting his establishment regularly. The man reluctantly admitted that Ayo was a regular and was in debt. Although recently he had paid off some of his debt, he was still losing. Now Ayo had a more difficult question; were drugs being sold in his establishment? There was a hesitation and Ayo pressed further and asked if the owner was selling drugs. The man was visibly shaken but exclaimed that he didn't sell drugs but that his patrons may well do so. Ayo then asked for a couple of names and the man could go. The man was visibly shaking as he left Ayo's office but he was glad to get out.

One of the names was a customer who used Ayo the deputy to clear goods. Now Mario's case was getting much larger. Ayo obtained a search warrant from a magistrate presenting some of the evidence and organised a search of the deputy's house as well as arresting the deputy and sealing his office. Ayo was present at the search and although the lady of the house protested, they headed straight for the deputy's bedroom. There they found some cash but more importantly in one of his coat pockets was a gold cigarette case. There were also a couple of packets of white powder hidden in a sock. Ayo thought it was too easy but he had to get Alicia to give a positive identification of the cigarette case.

Alicia identified the cigarette case and said Mario would never have given it to anyone. When challenged, Ayo the deputy said that Mario had given him the case. After a lot more questions and the revelation that the fingerprint on the ash tray was his, along with the presence of two packets of white powder in a sock, he finally confessed. He said he didn't know what he was doing after taking drugs in the morning. Ayo was satisfied and now they could get on with the funeral.

Later Ayo the deputy was found guilty and sentenced to death.

Arthur was going to the funeral service but dreading the drive and a friend came to his rescue. Graham was the manager of a construction company and knew Mario well. They had met at the club one Sunday and Mario had asked whether they had imported some big equipment recently. Graham had said they had received two large cranes at Lagos dock minus the cabins. Mario had seen the cabins at Apapa docks and they had big yellow markings. Graham was astonished as the ship's log hadn't recorded it docking at Apapa, only Lagos dock. Graham was eternally grateful to Mario and used him as clearing agent henceforth. Graham had a driver so Arthur and he could go to the funeral together. The driver would probably drive around until he found a parking place.

They went to Apapa and the church was packed, they had to stand at the back. Parking was impossible and the driver had to park almost in another suburb. As the coffin was moved towards the doors Arthur saw Alicia — she looked so serene. He nodded to her and she nodded back, and that was the last he saw of Alicia. The attendees seemed to be at least 70% Nigerian and nearly all the women were in tears. Alicia had Mario cremated and half his ashes scattered in Nigeria and the rest taken back to Sicily.

In the next few weeks there were several drug busts at the docks and the airport. One clearing agent was arrested and the dock became overcrowded with unclaimed merchandise. With two clearing offices closed the others couldn't cope. The military governor of Lagos State pronounced that if the goods were not cleared in two weeks the army would clear them. He put a colonel in charge of clearing the dock and when the two weeks were up everyone was expecting army trucks to take the goods to another location. The 'Mad Colonel' had other ideas and brought two bulldozers to shove the offending items into the sea. Henceforth no ships could dock at that side of the port.

Thursday Drama

"What a bloody mess this place is, paradise spoilt by the people. They couldn't lead an old horse to a knacker's yard. Most of the time I can't believe what I'm seeing and I've only been here five days." John was talking to a couple of new friends in the bar of the Ikeja Airport Hotel. "Most of the workers in my factory are thieves from the manager on down. They produce an enormous amount of scrap and it all disappears. I'm going to put a stop to that. Cheating bastards."

John was forty but looked thirty, except for his bald head. He worked out regularly in the gym and although not tall he was very well built. He worked hard and played hard but this was his toughest assignment. Carpentry, particularly furniture building was his line and his boss in Manchester had suggested he apply for this well-paid job in Africa. Being unmarried with few real ties in the UK he decided to give the "world" a try. The money looked good and this was an opportunity he couldn't miss. His visions and fantasies had disintegrated when he set foot in Nigeria. He was not prepared for the problems he found and the money was about half of what he would require. Anyway, he was stuck as his boss had taken his passport to get a proper work permit; he couldn't leave as he had arrived on a one-way ticket.

Tonight, in the airport hotel bar he was getting drunk on Star beer which he thought was the only good thing in Nigeria. "Only five days… only five days" he kept repeating. "These five days I have seen more than in the last five years and none of it good." John's speech was starting to slur and he was repeating himself more often. His young companions were enjoying John's company. It was their first trip to Nigeria and they were leaving soon and inwardly feeling sorry for John.

About midnight they all decided that was enough of cold Star and they unsteadily weaved their way to the door. The bar was air conditioned and they had grown accustomed to the temperature and reduced humidity but when they stepped outside it was like being wrapped up in a hot wet blanket. John felt sick but he took a deep breath and the feeling subsided. Poor Mike, one of his young companions, was not so lucky; he threw up over the path leading them to their rooms. John decided to leave the stricken pair and head for his room. Mike was propped up against a pillar and his friend Chris was getting greener by the minute.

John entered his room and flopped on the bed; he could still see and smell Mike's vomit. Then the musty smell of the room came through and he got up to switch on the air conditioner. The throbbing sound soon lulled him to sleep.

At 8 a.m. the next morning John awoke with a splitting headache. The thought of breakfast in the Hungry Man made his stomach churn. Whoever named the restaurant the Hungry Man was correct, you went in hungry and came out hungry, as the food was not good and the service even worse. What he needed was a drink, he was so parched. The shower helped then he made his way to the bar to get a soft drink.

Seated at the bar was an expat in uniform having a beer — so early in the morning? John sat down and ordered a soft drink. "Are you a pilot and if so what are you doing having a beer at 8 a.m.?" John asked impolitely but in a pleasant tone.

"Yes, to your first question and hair of the dog to your second. I see you have the same problem as me only a different solution." The pilot had a thick Scottish accent and after his answer introduced himself as Sammy from Aberdeen. John finished his first soft drink and ordered a second as this was much better than breakfast in the Hungry Man.

"Are you flying today?"

"No there is a problem with the aircraft — it happens all the time. They get you at the airport at six in the morning, leave you waiting for ninety minutes then tell you what they have known since the previous night. To them it's a game but today I'm the winner. I took my car to the airport so I didn't have to wait for transport. Now I'm free for the day and some poor passengers are waiting in the north for their Nigerian

Airways flight, they probably will not tell them till the afternoon that the flight has been cancelled. Tomorrow there will be chaos but then Nigerian Airways seems to thrive on chaos." John listened almost spell-bound, this was the first "old hand" he had spoken to and he was reinforcing the feelings he had about the place.

It was nine o'clock and John got up to leave, and as he did so, asked whether Sammy would be in the bar in the evening. "Very rarely come here for a drink except the occasional morning beer. I go to the Country Club. If you would like to come, I'll pick you up here at seven."

"Yes please." John thanked Sammy and left to find his driver. His hangover had almost gone and he was in high spirits after finding a new friend.

The day passed quickly without too much shouting, unlike the previous day. The hangover had not quite gone and John had threatened to kick several workers "up the arse" but this day his bark was worse than his bite. The workers were starting to fall into line but his major problem was, Friday, the foreman. This little fellow had resisted John at every chance. John had tested his knowledge of carpentry and Friday knew his stuff, but every order that John gave was changed or an extra order added on to the original. Sometimes this made smooth working impossible.

John had ordered that every spoilt piece of wood should be examined by John or Friday before it was taken to the scrap heap. Friday added that the piece should be left on the machine to be examined where the accident happened. John soon found that work was almost at a standstill while pieces were waiting to be examined and other workers were idle waiting for finished parts; John had to change the order. Another order similarly made work impossible; broken tools had to be reported and handed into the store for a replacement. Friday had them filling out accident reports before they could get new tools. As most of the men couldn't write or only write poorly some of the older more experienced hands spent their time filling out forms or dictating 'stories' of how the tools were broken.

This day John couldn't wait for work to end so he could visit the Country Club and mix with his own people — he was starting to notice how visible he was. He had expected locals to look at him because he was different but the constant stares occasionally unnerved him. At work he was the only white man, but he was in charge, whereas out on the street or sometimes in the hotel he was a little apprehensive. Tonight, would be different; the Country Club sounded a posh place.

John was talking to himself about the potential that this evening presented when Friday entered his office.

"What?" said Friday.

"Oh, I was just composing a letter,' said John hoping that was convincing the little bugger.

"The men would like to leave ten minutes early at night and come ten minutes early in the morning, as they are having problem with transport," said Friday with a grin.

"Okay." John was inwardly pleased at leaving early but they were probably leaving early anyway and not making up the time in the mornings. John started to ponder Friday's motives as the little man left the office with a big smile. "Had he suspected that I wanted to leave early? I must not be too quick to let them have what they want in future," John was talking to himself again. It was becoming a habit that had only started in Nigeria.

At a quarter to seven John was seated at the bar all dressed up for the Country Club. Sammy walked in and smiled as he approached John. "I would leave your jacket in your room you'll spoil it with sweat. Get rid of the tie as they are only worn on special occasions in the lounge. Dress codes although supposedly in force are normally ignored these days." John felt a little offended but he would not ignore the advice of his new friend.

They left the hotel after about ten minutes minus tie and jacket but having consumed one Star beer each. As they went to the car park John was excited but he visibly frowned as he climbed into Sammy's beat-up Toyota. Sammy laughed as he saw the frown "I would be a fool to have a good car here; I have a Jag in Aberdeen." This restored John's faith in his new friend and as they set off to the club, he found his spirits rising.

Sammy was a slow, careful driver who tried to avoid almost every pot hole, which was almost impossible in a road, nicknamed Crater Lane. John wondered if Sammy drove his planes the same way but that was not his main preoccupation; he was impatient to get to this club. As they pulled into the car park he was as excited as a child with a new toy. At first glance the building looked impressive but as they walked towards the entrance John could see that the weather and poor workmanship gave the place a dirty, ill-kept look.

Sammy signed in his guest and they entered a large hall where some members were playing badminton. This is more like it, thought John, who was feeling the need for some exercise. Sammy frowned "Energetic, sweaty buggers playing a stupid game." John thought otherwise but kept silent. There was a quick tour of the club and John was ushered into Sammy's favourite room, the snooker room. John's preliminary impressions were that most rooms needed a coat of paint. He had not been shown the grounds as it was too dark but was informed that there was a swimming pool, tennis and squash courts. Sammy told John the only well air-conditioned room was the snooker room and that was the reason for the quick tour.

John soon found that Sammy was the best player in the club and after two defeats decided to let someone else have a go. The snooker room was smoky and he wanted to have a walk around the club. As he left the snooker room he was hit by the hot humid air and a musty smell which he had not noticed before. The smell seemed to be a mixture of spilt beer and stale sweat. As he walked through the bar the beer smell was more apparent. There were no women in the bar and he later found out it was called the Cad's Bar. In the bar there were men of all colours energetically drinking or talking, with a couple playing darts. No one spoke to him as he walked through the bar and he next went through double doors into what was called The Lounge. Here there were soft seats covered with faded fabric but at least it looked more comfortable than the Spartan furniture in the bar. John could never resist having a professional look at the furniture and Nigeria had been a disappointment in that regard, even the stuff made in his factory would make a craftsman cringe.

The lounge room was full of both men and women and seemed more friendly than the bar or snooker room. John decided to stand at the bar and observe for a while. He was slightly disappointed that none of the members seemed interested in this new face. The members looked sort of ordinary, not the "colonials" he had expected. There seemed to be a lot more Nigerian members than he had expected and they were better dressed. John ordered another beer and decided to take a look outside. From the lounge he walked to a dimly lit patio where he found a few members sitting on stone seats at square stone tables. It was much more pleasant outside except there was no view. There was no moon and the grounds were just a bunch of shadows. John thought how dark it was after sunset, during the day it was bright and sunny but the sun went down fast, bringing on the blackness. John had to jerk himself back to reality as he was sinking into morbidity and homesickness.

A heavily accented voice from the shadows bought John back to reality. "May I join you?"

"Yes." replied John without thinking. The member sat down and introduced himself with a name John immediately forgot. They chatted for a while and John found out the man was a Syrian but more importantly he was the membership secretary. John was thinking of joining the club but the fees seemed high. The Syrian suggested that John's employer might be persuaded to pay the fees as the contacts in the club could bring in new business. There were also members in the club who might be able to supply items needed in the factory. John was to find out later that this worked with the owner who paid the fees without protest.

John's normal suspicion of foreigners was forgotten as he listened to this charming Arab's stories. Finally, John looked at his watch and decided that Sammy may have left, so he excused himself and made his way to the snooker room. Sammy was still playing and had not noticed John's absence. After the game John sat with Sammy and told him of his meeting with the membership secretary.

"That little crook. Do not get close to him, one of these days the Nigerians will lock him up or deport him." Sammy would not say anything else about the Syrian and after that the conversation was a bit stunted.

On the drive back to the hotel John was thinking that Sammy was going to fly tomorrow and had to be at the airport by 6 a.m. — best of luck to the passengers.

John joined the club and spent most of his evenings and weekends there. He saw a lot more of the Syrian than of Sammy and he made his first Syrian friend. Time in Nigeria started to pass quickly and John became more relaxed at work until one Thursday afternoon.

John was standing out on the veranda thinking about his coming leave and wondering if he would return. It was late afternoon and everything seemed peaceful when suddenly a young man came running through the gate and flung himself behind the veranda wall. John was taken aback and stepped towards the door.

"Please, sir, hide me," was the cry from the frightened man.

"Why?" said John.

"I have just had an accident and a little girl ran into my truck." John didn't quite know what to do but he then started to see a crowd pouring through the gate. "They will lynch me, you must stop them."

This young fellow had good English and didn't sound like a truck driver. John realised he had to do something, so at the top of his voice he shouted, "Stop. This is private property." The crowd did stop and probably the only word they understood in his sentence was "Stop".

A voice came from the crowd: "We want the driver. He killed our daughter."

As this was all happening Friday came onto the veranda and whispered something to the driver. At this point John told Friday to call the police.

Friday's reply was "I will, sir, but we must save this man — they will kill him." John realised he had to stall so he put his hands in the air and asked if someone speaking English could tell him what happened. As he guessed, several people started speaking at once, so again he told them to stop and only one person to tell the story. Two men came forward and John picked one of them. He told, that the girl had been chasing a chicken that had escaped and ran into the road as the truck came around the corner and killed her. While this was going on Friday came back and said he had spoken to the police and they would soon come. Friday had also sent the company driver to find policemen. John was pleased and thanked him for his quick thinking. When the first man had finished his story, he asked the second man his version. The second story was basically the same as the first and the crowd was getting restless. John told them this was a police case and that the man would be handed over to the police. The crowd was not happy but John folded his arms in a defiant stance.

As this stalemate was taking place the driver returned with two policemen. John pointed to the police and told the crowd to disperse, but realising that "disperse" was a word they might not understand he shouted, "Go away."

The crowd still wanted blood but luckily a police car pulled into the compound. With four more police present the crowd started to disperse but they were not happy. John was sweating and breathing heavily but he was pleased with himself and a group of workers standing behind him were also pleased. He had not noticed them but they were standing guard behind him. Friday was really grateful and thanked John as the police took the driver away.

Back in the office John poured several glasses of water down his dry throat and put the air conditioner on full blast. Friday came in and told John that he had saved the son of a chief from Enugu. Friday and several workers were from that region and they were all very happy. John had thought that Friday was a Yoruba from Lagos and had never thought where the work force was born. He found out that most of the better craftsmen were Ibo and they had moved from Biafra after the war to Lagos to find work. Many of them had gone to Catholic Schools and so their English was quite good. This was the first time John and Friday had chatted about anything but work. It was time to leave work but all the workers waited for John to leave his office and started clapping. John was taken aback by this demonstration and said so to Friday. Friday's answer was: "Everything will now run smoothly in the factory and we'll make the best furniture."

A couple of weeks passed and the factory was turning out more furniture in one week than they had turned out in two previously. The owner was very pleased and promised John an increase in salary, if he would come back after his leave which was fast approaching. Friday and a couple of the older hands had come up with new designs and John realised that these guys had been craftsmen before the war.

One afternoon John was sitting on the veranda with Friday discussing the coming week's schedule when two large Mercedes cars pulled into the compound. Several men got out of the cars and one tall man in a flowing gown (an Agbada) approached the veranda. Friday stood up and bowed and John frowned. The man introduced himself as the driver's father and he had come to thank John for saving his son. He explained that his son didn't normally drive a truck but he had picked the truck up from a mechanic to drive back to Enugu. Friday was offering the chief a seat but the chief refused as he had been siting too long in the car. The problem had been sorted out with the police and compensation had been paid to the dead girl's family. He was here to invite John and Friday to Enugu to celebrate the rebirth of his son. John thought that a curious phrase but in a sense it was correct. Friday was shaking with excitement but John asked, "How will we get there?"

"An air-conditioned Mercedes is at your disposal, of course, with a driver. I'm buying plenty of furniture from your factory and the owner has agreed to let you go for a week. Please come and see somewhere other than Lagos."

Friday was beside himself, this chief was saying, "Please". John agreed and the shook hands. This was a first.

The drive to Enugu was long and John slept most of the way but Friday couldn't sleep he was so happy. They arrived at Enugu and drove up to a huge house — in England it would have been a large mansion. They were greeted by drummers and Friday explained that an honoured guest was to receive all he desired. John met the driver, Nkiruku, who said, "Call me Kiru." And they chatted about his escape. The party that night went on until dawn and John had given up long before that hour. The next day they were taken around the estate and for the first time John had seen rural Nigeria. The chief had a fleet of trucks supplying agricultural products, mainly to Lagos. The second party seemed to be bigger than the first and John was enjoying the music, the dancing and the beer.

Back in Lagos, with two days before his leave Friday asked, "Will you come back?"

"Yes, I fancy one of those girls in Enugu."

Nigerian Trilogy
Part 1 An Interesting Job

"Robert, we may have an interesting job for you." An interesting job in the civil service? Could there be such a thing? thought Robert.

Behind the desk was a balding, rotund man of about fifty speaking with a BBC-type voice. The office was wood paneled with several paintings and a large photo of the Queen on the wall behind the desk.

Robert had worked in the civil service since leaving school in Liverpool with a few O-levels. Currently he was working in the unemployment office (the old Labour Office) in the centre of Manchester. A few weeks earlier he had applied for a transfer; he was getting fed-up with whining, often lying patrons. After hearing nothing he assumed his application had either been turned down or gotten lost. It was a bit of a surprise to be offered an interview in London, and they even enclosed a rail voucher and a voucher for a hotel. It seemed strange that there was no address for the interview and the letterhead on the offer was an administrative centre in Glasgow. He was to be met at the railway station and taken directly to the interview; all he would need was a change of clothes for the next day. Robert showed the letter to his wife who was suspicious. "Well, if there is any problem, they will throw me off the train," said Robert laughingly.

There was no problem on the train and he was met at the station by a young well-dressed man who drove him to the office. Robert had enquired of the young man to what office he was being taken. The driver, who didn't give his name, said he was only a driver and only knew the address. Robert had been a bit surprised how quickly the driver had identified him at the station. He had introduced himself with a hand shake in his fairly thick Liverpudlian accent but the young man had only said, "Let's go."

The drive was quite short and Robert had seen very little of interest on this his first visit to London. They stopped at a building which looked like a well-kept block of flats, nothing like the flats near where he lived in Manchester. There was no sign on the office where he was taken by the driver and another surprise was that the secretary was a man. Robert was now starting to wonder what all this was about, a myriad of thoughts were pounding his brain, when he was ushered into the office.

This was the strangest interview, after the interesting job bit the man had told him everything was sanctioned by the civil service bosses and Robert should have a bit of travelling to do. Firstly, he was to work for a short time in a factory near Birmingham. Accommodation was provided and he could take Dorothy with him if he wished. His salary would be the current salary with certain (unspecified) allowances and if he didn't like the job, he could go back to his current position. After the stay in Birmingham, he would be transferred to a factory in Portsmouth as a temporary installation engineer.

"I'm no engineer."

"We know that, but you have good people skills and the job you'll have to do will not take much expertise, and anyway, we think you are a quick learner." Robert was rather pleased with that remark, and thought it best that he just listen and agree with the man whenever possible. That was more or less the end of the interview. Robert was handed an envelope and told to have a good evening in London. In the envelope was fifty pounds and a map of the area around his hotel. "This is not the way the civil service normally works, is it?" Robert said to himself as he walked to the waiting car. They pulled up at the hotel and as Robert got out of the car the driver (name still unknown) gave him an envelope. "I'll be here at nine o'clock tomorrow; enjoy your evening." Those were the same words as the interviewer said, which amused Robert.

The hotel was nothing special but the room was large with a double bed and a TV. The toilet and bathroom were down the hallway but there was no phone. Robert opened the envelope and read the letter. It said that the interview was confidential and that Robert could only discuss it with his wife and possibly his mother. In his future work no one was to know that he worked for the civil service and if he agreed to this, he should sign the letter and give it to the driver in the morning. The letter was brief and the letterhead was again from the office in Glasgow. This was not the kind of letter that Robert would expect from his employer but he signed it anyway. He wanted to tell Dorothy but that would have to wait till tomorrow as there was no phone at home in Manchester.

Suddenly he felt hungry, it was lunchtime and he had the rest of the day to see London. What would he do with an extra fifty pounds in his pocket? He soon found out that prices in London were much higher than in Manchester and the extra money was not going to allow him to buy Dorothy an expensive present. After a sandwich for lunch and walking most of the day he found a colourful umbrella for Dorothy. He saw a few sights and went back to the hotel to have a lie down. He was still mulling over the interview and trying to make sense of making him an engineer.

The evening meals in the hotel were not covered by the voucher but luckily there would be a free breakfast in the morning. He retired to the nearest pub for fish and chips and a pint. This was a good pub with most of the patrons wearing suits with ties; the fish and chips were a bit expensive but the beer was double the price of Manchester. Robert was not a big drinker and one pint was enough. While eating and drinking he was still trying to make sense of the day's happenings. Everything was so cut and dried and unusual for the service, it was brief, even the letter of acceptance had no clauses outlining conditions and benefits. Maybe they want me to spy on workers collecting unemployment and still working. Or maybe they want me to spy on the factory owners. This line of thought seemed the most plausible, that is why they are sending me out of Manchester. It was curious that the man had said he could discuss it only with Dorothy and his mother. Did they know he had a father who had gone missing many years ago? As he walked back to the hotel, he knew he was going to be a spy.

The next day the driver picked him up and relieved him of the letter; the drive to the station was in complete silence. At the station the driver wished him the best of luck. The train seemed to take an age to get to Manchester and throughout the journey Robert could only think of what this was going to mean in the future.

Dorothy was waiting at the station with a multitude of questions: Had he got the job? Where was the job? How much was the pay? When did the job start? Robert could only answer that he assumed he had the job and the pay was the same. Dorothy didn't say anything more as she could see Robert seemed confused. After a little while Dorothy was surprised to hear that they were to move to Birmingham and Robert was to become an engineer. She would have to give up her job but the prospect of later moving to Portsmouth was a bonus. As a young girl her family had often taken holidays on the south coast and she loved having the sea close.

The move to Birmingham went without a hitch; they were met at New Street station and driven to a house in Solihull (one of the better suburbs). They were to live in the top of a house and the apartment was fully furnished. Robert started to worry about the rent but their driver said it would come out of expenses. Dorothy was just gazing at the kitchen which was modern, well laid out and large, so spacious it was nearly as big as their flat in Manchester. The driver's words on parting were that he would pick Robert up at eight in the morning.

Next morning Robert was picked up at eight sharp and driven to an industrial estate. The driver informed him that this company specialised in making machinery parts. They had some of the best lathes and presses available. Robert had no specific job but was to observe everything and get to know how to use the machinery. "Take your time, get to know the workforce and try to make friends" the driver advised. He also handed Robert a package which contained a map, bus timetables and a quarterly bus pass. This was a second 'driver' who couldn't be a normal driver, thought Robert. On entering the factory Robert was ushered to the office which overlooked most of the work area. The whole place was much cleaner than he had expected and much of the machinery seemed almost new. The manager introduced himself as David — Robert was later to learn that David was part owner. "We make a lot of specialty machine parts many of which are one-offs and the orders come from all over the world. You'll start work with Bill who operates one of our older lathes, you'll note that all scrap is immediately binned and each operator keeps his machine as clean as possible. Cleanliness, precision and safety are our main concern here."

Bill was an older man with a strong Scottish accent who continued to work while chatting away at a great rate. Robert had to listen quite intently for a while to get used to the accent, but Bill was a good teacher. The first day passed very quickly and his next problem was how to get home. Bill and his mates showed Robert the bus stop and asked him if he would like a beer. Robert excused himself as Dorothy was all alone and he had not been able to contact her.

The bus ride was quite short and the driver politely informed him when he should get off. The map now came in useful and he arrived at the flat in about five minutes. Dorothy was waiting in the lounge watching TV.

"We must get a phone."

"We have one," she replied. "What we don't have is much food; we need to go shopping. This kitchen is unreal, it was spotless but I have cleaned it twice and this sofa is so comfortable I have had forty winks at least twice today."

Life in Solihull was comfortable and with no rent and a free phone provided they could enjoy an occasional night out and save some money. Dorothy soon got to enjoy her leisurely life and found people friendly and helpful. Robert's mother visited and was astounded by the flat; she lived in a small, two-bedroom house in Liverpool and this flat was bigger than her house. Robert decided not to tell his mother about the job, in fact he rarely talked even to Dorothy about his work. His work was progressing well and he was popular with the workers and the manager. Robert had used all the machinery by the time the three months were up. When it was time to leave, he realised this had been the best working environment he could ever expect, in fact if they had offered him a job he would have been sorely tempted to stay.

Before his time was up he was summoned to London and everything proceeded as before except that a different man interviewed him. This interviewer was more formal and had the manner of an ex-military man. After a few preliminaries about his work in Birmingham Robert was surprised when the interview took a surprising turn. "Where is your father?"

"I don't know. He left when I was young. All that I know is that he is Nigerian and a sailor, I think a stoker."

"Yes, that is true. He comes from Port Harcourt in Nigeria and is still a sailor working on trading ships around Africa." Robert detected a little edge in the man's voice as he said "sailor", he was also surprised that they knew about his father. "Would you react favourably to being sent to Nigeria after your stint in Portsmouth?"

"Yes." Robert was trying to disguise the surprise and elation in his voice.

"Right, in Portsmouth you'll learn how to fit and use some machinery much of it associated with the maritime industry. After your time in Portsmouth, you'll be sent to Lagos to fit some machines in a factory. Make sure you and Dorothy have passports."

That seemed to be the end of the interview and Robert was not offered the opportunity to ask any questions. The man just rose, offered his hand and said, "Good luck."

Dorothy was loath to leave Birmingham and the beautiful flat and was almost in tears as they caught the train to London.

"Why are we going to London?"

"I have to pick up some instructions and house keys."

"We are going to live in a house? How big?"

"I don't know, all I know is that we'll spend a couple of nights at no expense and you can see some of the sights."

That cheered Dorothy up as she had not been to London before and she suddenly became quite excited. Robert was less excited, he was trying to think what they wanted from him. He had prepared a short, written report of his Birmingham job. He couldn't identify any fiddles, the workers seemed to be all honest and the small amount of waste was quite outstanding. The boss was a great bloke always available with advice but not pushy. Robert had never heard him raise his voice; in fact, he would often join the workers for morning tea and just be one of the group. Robert had not seen the books, so he couldn't say anything about finances but he had seen work come in, efficiently dealt with and dispatched immediately.

They reached London and were met at the station and taken to their hotel which was slightly more up-market from his first visit to London. The driver would pick him up at nine and promised to have him back by eleven. In the evening they went to a restaurant and had a slap-up meal — Robert had saved money in Birmingham and thought Dorothy deserved a treat.

The next day he was taken to a different office and was confronted by two men, both in identical dark brown suits with purple ties. Robert thought they looked a bit comical but suppressed his smile.

"Robert your report from Birmingham is very good and you now have a working knowledge of machinery. Now you are going to fit machinery and this job will be a bit dirtier. For your trouble you'll get an increase in salary." That is good news thought Robert. "Your house will be in a more working-class neighbourhood but you'll probably be there only about three months. Make sure you get the change of address on your driver's licence and carry it with you at all times to identify yourself. You may go out to ships in the harbour and the local police are often suspicious of small boats visiting foreign ships. We don't want you visiting police stations or attracting any untoward attention. Portsmouth, around the dock area, can be quite an aggressive place and although we know you are a sober young man, we don't think it wise you visit any of the local pubs."

Just one of the men was doing the talking the other sat in silence.

"Here are the keys to the house and the address, it's fully furnished and stocked for a few days. Take a taxi from the station and have a week off. You'll be contacted and taken to work on your first day and from then on you are on your own. Learn as much as you can both inside and outside the factory. You'll need overalls as this job will be a bit dirtier."

With that the interview ended and both men got up and left the room. Robert sat for a second or two thinking what to do, but his thought were interrupted by the driver entering the room and offering him a ride to the hotel.

"Dorothy, I have just had the strangest interview. No one let me speak and I was dying to ask a few questions but it was obvious I was just there to listen. I'm working for a strange bunch." Robert described the two men and told her almost everything they, or at least one of them, had said. "He said 'dirty' twice but the good thing is that I get a raise in salary, we can save for our own place."

Arriving at the house they realised that this working-class area was a cut above what they knew from Liverpool and Manchester. They had spent a quite tiring one-and-a-half days in London seeing all the normal sights and Tower Bridge had impressed Robert the most. He was starting to look at things in engineering terms and he was a little surprised that three months had changed him so much.

The next week they spent exploring Portsmouth. Dorothy suggested they go to the Isle of Wight but Robert said they could do that one weekend when they had found their way around. He slightly surprised himself — before going to Birmingham he would have been up for anything. They had a look around the Portsmouth Polytechnic and Dorothy saw a course in Word Processing on a computer. She was a good typist and thought it would be good to learn how to use a computer as it might be useful when she had to get a job. Robert said they could afford it especially with the raise he had just received and he thought it a good idea for Dorothy to have something to do when he was at work. The polytechnic was just about within walking distance but there was also a good bus service in their area. During the week they often spent a lot of time near the harbour. Dorothy loved to be near the sea and Robert started to take an interest in the ships. Sunday evening was spent at a good restaurant and Robert spent most of the time thinking about his new job. When he went to Birmingham, he had been happy-go-lucky but now he was more serious.

On Monday morning at eight a driver arrived to take him to work with a letter and a bus pass for three months. Robert decided to watch where they were going and read the letter later. The driver talked about their route and pointed out a bus that Robert might take on the way home. They pulled up at a factory gate and the driver pointed out the office. Robert walked to the office putting the letter in his pocket as he went. In the office he met a lady he assumed was the secretary — he was later to learn that she was the personnel manager. She greeted him with a smile.

"You must be our new recruit. You'll need overalls I hope we have some your size." Robert tried a few overalls until he found one his size, not exactly new but in good shape. The lady introduced herself as Mrs. Jones and proceeded to call for Bill on the loud speaker. Another Bill thought Robert.

This Bill was an older man but not fat and balding; he was lean and wiry with a good tan. Mrs. Jones informed Robert that he would be working with Bill, as his assistant, and that Bill fixed machinery in the factory and fitted it outside. Bill showed Robert around the factory and they ended up at a work bench where Bill was fixing the motor of a pump. Robert watched and handed Bill tools when he needed them. At about ten they went to have morning tea and sat down at a long table in the canteen with six other men. Robert was quiet, assessing the situation. These blokes were not as friendly as the Birmingham workers and from their tone he sensed some tension. Finally, one of the men at the end of the table asked, "How did you get this job?"

Robert thought the best thing to say was the approximate truth,

"I don't actually know, I was working in a machine shop in Birmingham and was told to come here to this job." The questioner made a grunt but didn't probe further. After tea Bill told Robert to take no notice as, John, the man who asked the question, wanted Robert's job, Bill noticed that they did some work with the Birmingham factory and often received machined parts from them so maybe they had some kind of relationship. The first day went smoothly and Robert found the correct bus to the end of his street. After a week of getting to know the area, he felt comfortable about the travel home.

Dorothy was waiting with his tea and then they discussed the day's events. Dorothy was excited about the course she was taking and she thought the days of the typewriter were numbered. Robert was telling Dorothy that the workers at the factory were going to be more difficult to get to know compared with the men in Birmingham. "I'll have to use a bit of Liverpool humour and see how that goes down."

In the next two weeks Robert became more popular at work and with one exception all the workers were laughing at his jokes. Work with Bill was enjoyable and varied but what Robert wanted was to get a look at some of the ships. Bill explained that the worst job was fixing petrol pumps in garages — there was always spilt petrol and every job was urgent and had to be fixed as fast as possible. Robert was to see this at the end of the second week when there was a call from a garage with old style pumps. Luckily Bill had worked on this pump before and had a replacement. The job was still messy and Robert felt sick with the smell of the petrol leaking as they replaced the pump. Bill let Robert move away from the job a few times to get his breath. "At least we are in the open on this job but the next job might be in a closed environment and even I have to take a breather some times." At the start of the third week, they got a job on a ship, and fortunately it was a water pump. They arrived at the harbour where a small boat was waiting to take them out to an old tanker. Robert was excited but also a little apprehensive as they would have to climb a rope ladder and Robert was not a good swimmer. At least the tools were taken in a basket and Robert was thinking that he would have liked to have been taken aboard in the same manner. Even though this was a water pump it was a bilge pump and Robert tried to ignore the smell in the confined area in which they had to work. He was thinking if this boat started rocking, he would have trouble keeping his breakfast down. Robert was glad to finish the job and get off the ship, now he knew why he had received a raise.

In the next few months, they worked on several ships and it always seemed they were not docked at the quay but out in the harbour. Robert got used to the smells and layout of the engine rooms and enjoyed most of the work except working on old oil pumps. They were stopped once by the Harbour Police but when Bill introduced Robert as his mate no questions were asked. Bill was known all over the area and all the seamen including the captains treated him with respect. Robert was allowed to go to some jobs on his own and he really enjoyed the feeling of elation he had when a job was completed successfully. On one occasion they were called to a navy ship to fix a pump. This was something new and Bill said it didn't happen often so it must be a difficult job, and it was. The pump was almost inaccessible and it took almost all morning to remove it. Robert was thinking whoever designed this engine room must have been an idiot or maybe someone who never sailed in a ship. He amused himself by the thought that the designer was probably a civil servant. As the pump came out, they were invited to lunch in the canteen. Robert was taken aback by the quality and quantity of the food and said so to one of the sailors whose reply was, "This is muck compared with what they get in the officers mess." Robert thought he could eat this muck any day.

The job took the rest of the day and when they had finished the chief engineer invited them for a beer, he was so happy his team had not had to do this job. There was laughter when Robert asked if there was a suggestion box as he wanted to suggest rerouting the pipes to make the pump more accessible.

"The paperwork alone could take two weeks work and then there would be an enquiry chaired by some high-level civil servant. It could then take at least a year before anything could be done if they considered it a good idea. We could be at sea for a few months so nothing could happen for two years at least. I'm sorry son but the navy and civil service work in very slow ways their duty to perform." Robert chuckled to himself knowing the ways of the civil service, except of course the wing that currently employed him.

One Friday after about three months Mrs. Jones called him to the office. "We want you to go to Nigeria to help fit some machinery in our factory there. The first thing you have to do is go to London to the Nigerian Consulate. We have a letter for you to take so you can get a temporary work visa. This could take a little time and we expect you to come back to work for the time it takes to get the visa." Robert wanted to thank her but thought it better he just acted surprised. Bill had a good laugh when Robert told him the news.

"The last bloke who went there swore he had tried hell and was never going back. I understand the resident engineer is a strange bloke who must be hard-up for a job as he has stuck it for a while."

"Do you think I'll be there long?" asked Robert.

"The last bloke, Tom, was supposed to go for two weeks and spent nearly two months there, it seems there was a bit of a war going on." The other workers had a good laugh on hearing the news and John was particularly delighted as Tom had left the company within a few weeks of returning from Nigeria; maybe Robert would do the same.

Robert couldn't wait to tell Dorothy the news, but Dorothy had other news — Robert was to call a London number at ten on Saturday morning. So they do work at the weekend, thought Robert. The call was answered by a woman.

"Let us know what train you'll be catching and we'll pick you up." With that she said good morning and ended the call. Robert was a little taken aback by the shortness of the call and it seemed he was never destined to ask a question. This is a bloody funny organisation they don't give me a chance to know the next move and I, Robert, seem to be just a pawn. On the other hand, I'm having a good time and life is so easy there must be catch.

Robert caught the train to Waterloo Station and was picked up by a driver and taken to the Nigerian Consulate. The driver was not too communicative but did have one piece of advice: "Have lots of patience, you'll need it." On entering the consulate Robert noticed a rather large queue but they seemed to be waiting for their passports with visas. The empty counter was the one he approached and his applications were accepted with a nice smile and the encouraging advice: "Come back tomorrow."

Robert was out in less than three minutes and he greeted his driver with a smile of satisfaction. "That was pretty quick."

"Yes, a quick start and an untimed ending," was the driver's cryptic reply."

Robert was starting to enjoy his London excursions and the pub culture was starting to grow on him except that two pints of beer seemed to be his limit. One pub had a jukebox and the Jimi Hendrix and Jimmy Cliff discs produced a very happy feeling in Robert. He thought of his dad when the music was playing but afterwards, he felt a bit bad about the way his mother was treated. He would never treat Dorothy badly.

The next day at the consulate he joined the queue and was finally greeted with: "Come back tomorrow."

Robert tried to talk to the clerk but a friendly voice in the queue advised him that "Come back tomorrow" probably meant wait a few weeks. On emerging from the consulate, the driver advised that he should go back to Portsmouth and wait. On the train he mused that his contacts had not helped and he wondered why?

Dorothy listened to Robert as he let out his frustration and impatience with the visa business but she was not too excited about going to Nigeria, she was enjoying Portsmouth. The computer course was showing her possibilities of getting a better job when Robert's "adventure" was over. She could now approach any future employer with skills and a confidence she was previously lacking.

Robert spent the next two weeks with a sinking feeling; why was it taking so long? "His people" should be doing something to rush this through. The problem was he didn't know who to call. He thought the best thing was to talk to Mrs. Jones, she might know what was going on. Mrs. Jones said he should call her Anne and that the name was not to be used in the factory. Anne knew all about Robert and with a few tit-bits of information about his life Robert knew he had no secrets from her. Her major advice was that he should stay calm and let it all unfold; pushing things may arouse suspicion. This was not the first time operatives had been sent to Nigeria. The word "operative" stuck in Robert's mind. She explained that the consulate was slow but quite thorough, although the clerks and general staff were pretty hopeless the consul was very smart. "I think his family have a long history in the civil service, which was run by the British before 1960." She also explained that if his passport were lost there would be no problem in getting another passport for him and Dorothy.

"How could they lose my passport?" exclaimed Robert.

"Well, they could be propping up someone's desk or worse thrown out with the rubbish, but if they were thrown out with the rubbish, we would have them," Anne said with a broad smile. "Just carry on working as normal and don't let this bother you and you should not tell Dorothy about any of this conversation."

Robert was used to not telling Dorothy everything but had never been instructed to tell her nothing before. It bothered him that he couldn't decide what secret was to be kept from Dorothy but he came to the conclusion that Anne was the secret.

Two weeks passed and then a letter arrived to inform Robert that he should pick up his passport. He informed Anne but she seemed to know already. Anne would start the process of getting airline tickets and Robert should be ready to leave in one week.

Returning to Portsmouth with the passports Robert was in high spirits and he met Dorothy at the station with the greeting "We're off to Nigeria."

Dorothy was not so enthusiastic but she smiled and said,

"When?"

"In about a week," Robert was ecstatic.

"Isn't that a bit soon?" Dorothy lost her smile.

The week passed so fast Robert couldn't concentrate on anything but Nigeria. Each night he studied maps and any articles he could find on Nigeria. Dorothy was very quiet and stayed in the background.

The day before he was to finish work Anne called him to the office. "Here are your tickets — you are flying British Caledonian from Gatwick. You can go by train to Gatwick. When you are in Nigeria take things easy, our engineer is a difficult man but a good one. Take time to go to Port Harcourt and have a good look around. You can use the excuse that you want to see your father although I'm afraid you'll not find him. See a few relatives and listen to all the gossip you hear. Finally, have a good time."

The workers gave him a little send-off and Robert drank more than two beers, he was so looking forward to boarding British Caledonian.

Part 2 Lonely

Dennis was sitting alone at the table staring at his cold almost untouched dinner. It looked appetising but he had no appetite. Surrounding the plate were several empty beer bottles; their contents had depleted his appetite. He had stared at the plate for hours, occasionally shouting commands to the cook to "Bring another beer." It was a daily ritual that the cook knew well and no matter how he enticed and cajoled his master to eat, the result was always the same — untouched food surrounded by beer bottles. The little Ibo did his best but to no avail.

Dennis was tired, sick and depressed, so depressed he had contemplated suicide. He was lonely and yet every evening he avoided company. He couldn't rouse any enthusiasm for a visit to the Ikeja Club where he could drink and maybe enjoy a conversation with other lonely people. He hated it all — the country Nigeria, the climate and most of all the people. Work was a necessary drudge, an interlude between bed and booze. The work was boring and the workers lazy and insolent.

"Why am I here?" he kept asking himself.

As he sat at the dinner table every evening his thoughts were all in the past. There were some good, some bad memories but they were all infinitely better than his present reality. This cursed country was a living hell, a final nail in his coffin. Malaria had hit him twice and he had been conscientiously nursed by his cook-steward Johnson. The little fellow was the only shining light in a pool of doom. Dennis liked this diminutive Ibo but couldn't relate to him, but then he had never really tried. Dennis longed to put to sea in a big ship taking care of throbbing engines and receiving sharp commands from the captain. Alas those days were long gone and the nostalgia was eating him. He wished he could scream his contempt for the whole landlocked human race; he wanted to give them all shit. It was no use, if he did let it all out only Johnson would hear and he couldn't be expected to understand. This place had ground him down and was going to do so in the future.

Dennis rose unsteadily from his chair and staggered off towards his bedroom. He didn't care when he bumped into the coffee table and knocked it over, he only cursed as he fell against the wall. The mess would be cleaned up by Johnson and tomorrow would be the same painful routine. Dennis entered the bedroom and collapsed full length on the bed falling asleep without undressing.

The next morning the alarm woke him from a fitful sleep, he was covered in sweat and realised he had forgotten to switch on the air conditioner. Dennis changed his shirt but decided not to have a shower; who was he going to see? Just a crowd of Nigerian workers who smelt worse than him. He wandered into the kitchen and in a daze opened the fridge and reached for a beer. This was Star beer probably the most popular beer in Lagos, the first few gulps made him feel better, it seemed to clear the haze. Johnson stood and watched then plucked up the courage to ask, "Breakfast master?"

"No thanks, here is some money to buy another case of beer, get Star but if it not available buy Gulder." Dennis was always sending Johnson for beer which he obtained from the local market.

"How about food? We have no meat or vegetables,' was Johnson's timid reply.

"Bugger the food, just buy beer. I don't eat the food anyway."

The driver was waiting as Dennis staggered out into the sunlight after his second beer. He sat almost motionless in the back seat of the car oblivious of the mayhem around him that was Lagos traffic. Arriving at the gates of the factory he wanted to tell the driver to turn around and take him home but he suppressed that urge. He assumed that today was going to be like any other day, barking orders and inspecting working and broken machinery, but there was a surprise waiting for him on his desk.

Entering his office, he could see something in the middle of his otherwise bare desk. Dennis hated paperwork and tried to keep his desk clear just in case he needed a snooze. He slumped into his chair and stared at the telex for several seconds. He collected his thoughts and started to think what it could contain.

"Those idiots at head office in Portsmouth probably have some stupid query or suggestion," he said out loud and quickly looked around to check if anyone could have heard him. Whatever the telex had to say, he could do nothing he was only the engineer. The manager took care of everything, the manager was a crook with his finger on the pulse of all that was going on in the factory. The work force was insolent and lazy and would not take on any new ideas. Dennis finally reached for the telex and irritably tore open the envelope. The message was short but it put Dennis's head in a spin:

Robert Partridge arriving Thursday to fit new machinery, accommodate him and give him all necessary help to speedily complete his job.

"A speedy job in this country would be a miracle." Dennis was talking to himself again. After rereading the telex, he was perplexed — there was no new machinery in the factory and today was Tuesday. He cursed and walked down the corridor to the manager's office. He knocked and immediately opened the door. Jide, the manager, was seated at his desk writing something. The smell of sweet aftershave repelled Dennis; it reinforced the disgust and contempt he had for Jide.

"Here, read this," Dennis barked in a frustrated tone.

"Í already know, I received a telex yesterday, some new machinery is lying in Apapa docks and I'm writing a letter before customs lose it."

"Well, what do we do?"

"Meet him, put him up in your house and give him all the assistance he needs."

There was no love lost between these two, contempt for each other was the only thing they had in common. Dennis stood motionless for a second and the suddenly turned, left the office and slammed the door behind him. The manager's words had bought no protest only a grunt.

That was the first time in weeks Dennis and Jide had spoken to each other and the next day their normal practice returned with a memo from Jide to Dennis: *We'll both meet the new man at the airport.* The memo put Dennis in a really bad mood and so he left work early and got hammered at home. The next morning, he showered and felt really terrible. He had a nagging ache in the left side of his lower back and suspected it was his kidneys. He put on clothes he had not worn for months, had a shave and as he emerged Johnson said he looked smart.

Living near the airport was an advantage on this day, the traffic was light and Dennis reached the airport early. At least the new airport was air conditioned not like the hole that was the old airport. Dennis had arrived a year ago and had been ushered into a place worse than any dock area he had visited in the navy. It was a hot, sticky, overcrowded shed. That first impression was to be reinforced as he started to live in Lagos.

The navy had been a good life but they had forced him to retire and the only job he could get was in this sweat-box. One year of hate, from the very first minute, had taken its toll. His self-esteem had almost vanished and now he was waiting for some bright-eyed whizz kid. The thought of having to accommodate this interloper was playing on his mind, he imagined a tall slim blond man about thirty years old.

At the arrivals hall the driver was holding a piece of cardboard with *Robert Partridge* written in large red letters. He was showing it to every white man who passed. Suddenly a young man was animatedly pointing at the name and his chest. Dennis was taken aback; "He's black," he almost said audibly to himself.

"You are Robert Partridge?"

"Yes mate, you must be Dennis," came the answer in a strong Liverpudlian accent. Oh, meet my wife, Dorothy."

Dennis was startled. "Nobody told me about a wife, in fact, nobody actually told me about you."

Dorothy said hello in an even thicker accent and flashed him a delightful smile that almost melted Dennis, but he was still angry.

"Boy did I get *him* wrong!" Dennis said under his breath.

Crazy thoughts were passing through Dennis's brain. What would Johnson say? He would not like a woman messing about in his kitchen. What would she do while they were at work? Did she drink beer? Dennis shook himself and was back in reality staring at Robert and Dorothy. The driver mentioned something about the manager and this stirred Dennis into action.

"Let's go before that idiot manager arrives. He's always late, probably be late for his own funeral."

Robert laughed and cracked the ice again.

They drove to the house and Dennis hardly said a word, Robert spoke almost incessantly but Dorothy hardly said a word either except to comment that many of the other drivers probably never had a driving test. Dennis thought that was a polite way of putting the way they drove. Dennis listened most of the time but such a concentrated effort early in the morning was a problem. Can that boy talk! thought Dennis; His whole life story in a short car ride.

"I bet when you saw me you thought I was black, but I'm a half-caste," Robert said proudly. Dennis didn't remember anyone using that term with such pride before. Sailors use lots of terms for colour of skin but rarely was that term used. "My father was a sailor, a stoker on a tramp."

Dennis suddenly smiled, the first smile of the year, the mention of a sailor made a tingle pass down his spine. "My mother is Irish and she married this Nigerian from Port Harcourt, she got pregnant, had me, and then he disappeared. We haven't seen him for twenty years."

Dennis was now chuckling.

"I hear you was in the navy."

Dennis didn't get a chance to answer as Robert was off again: "I wanted to go to sea, maybe I could have found my old man, but my mother said a big no to that idea."

Now Dennis was openly laughing and only stopped when they pulled into the driveway.

"Wow! You live in this big house? I'm impressed." Even Dorothy was only able to get a few words of admiration out before Robert monopolised the conversation again.

Johnson appeared and Dennis detected slight displeasure at the sight of Dorothy, but he shook hands warmly with Robert. They entered the sparsely furnished house and Robert was aghast.

"What a space! Mi mom would love this she would be overpowered by all this space."

Dennis had never really noticed.

"We used to live in her two-up two-down poky little house; you could fit most of it in this living room." Dennis again smiled, he had not heard that expression for years, in fact Robert used a lot of dated expressions and Dennis was glad to hear them.

The next few weeks changed Dennis's life. He started to eat more, drink less and smile more. Work was no longer a drudge and every morning the trip to work was full of Robert's stories. Dorothy did drink beer and enjoyed Star in moderation; she confided in Dennis that Robert couldn't handle too much beer. Dennis reassured Dorothy that he would look after Robert and make sure he never got drunk. It gave him a good feeling that he was seen by Dorothy as a personal friend — he couldn't remember the last time a woman had confided in him. Robert also liked Star beer but admitted himself that he couldn't handle it. "I'll be no good to Dorothy if I drink too much of this."

Dennis was feeling like a father figure and he liked it although it was new to him. Johnson had a few rough days with Dorothy in the kitchen, but when Dorothy admitted that he was the better cook he beamed widely and shook his head from side to side with pleasure. Johnson had been a cook in colonial times and showed Dorothy some of his recipes. He was very pleased when Dorothy said she would try some of his recipes when she got back to England. She also told him he could do all the cooking while they were in Lagos, she would live like a lady of leisure.

Johnson took Dorothy to the market but politely asked her to stand well away while he did the bargaining. The only thing she disliked was to watch the butchers smash the meat with an axe and she gracefully declined when offered cooked bush rat. The market mommas were intrigued by her long blonde hair and several giggled when they touched it but she never felt threatened in the market and quite enjoyed the weekly trips.

Robert was good at work. He soon found the measure of the manager and agreed with Dennis that the man was a crook. That pleased Dennis, as he had known it from the first time he started work in Lagos. The workers liked Robert and Dennis's duties became easier. The new machinery was taking a long time to clear and so they had plenty of time to enjoy Lagos. They went to the club nearly every night and to the beach at the weekend. Dennis hated to be out in the midday sun but he would sit in the shade, watching, smelling and feeling the sea. He wondered why he had never gone to the beach before Robert arrived. Dennis stared long and hard at the ships in the roads waiting to get into harbour. Dreaming past memories became a pleasure and he even told Robert and Dorothy some stories. Mostly he told stories to Dorothy when Robert was absent. Robert decided to go to Port Harcourt for a few days to trace his father and that gave both Dennis and Dorothy a chance to do all the talking.

Initially Dennis's stories were about his life in the navy but he was able to admit how unhappy he had been in Lagos before their arrival. Dorothy was quiet when he finally opened up and there were tears in her eyes when he mentioned suicide. When she told Robert, he took it easier. "I can see how lonely you could get in this place, he is not as out-going as me." That was a majestic understatement.

At last, it was time for Dorothy and Robert to leave and Dennis felt a deep foreboding. Dorothy had been a sounding board and a fantastic listener. Robert had been an inspiration in the way he dealt with every situation. The workers were a new bunch, they came on time, worked to orders and smiled. The manager was quiet when Robert was around, maybe he was being careful because he was scared Robert would let head office know the true situation.

Robert had finished his work although it had taken much longer than anticipated. Head office had notified him that he should come home. Dennis watched Dorothy and Robert pack up their things and Johnson had a very unhappy face that even Dennis detected. Johnson presented Dorothy with a small carved ebony figure and hoped she would be reminded of him when she looked at it. Dorothy was overwhelmed and promised it would have pride of place on the mantle shelf above the fire place. When she tried to explain "mantle" Johnson said he had been in houses in colonial times that had fire places although he had never seen one used.

On the last evening they spent at home Robert was in an excitedly talkative mood. He almost reviewed all the work at the factory and said a little about Port Harcourt.

"You know when I arrived at the airport and they asked me for my passport, I told the officer I had just come from Lagos — the same country. He was being a bit difficult until I told him my surname and then it was all smiles."

"Enjoy your stay in Port Harcourt and find plenty of relatives," the officer said as he let me go. "I did find some distant relatives and found out my father was a bit of a hero in the area, but no one knew where I could find him."

Dennis casually said, 'I wonder why?' and then regretted he had said it.

The conversation (only Robert was really talking) turned to England and his voice showed he was obviously excited.

"You may know I have made a lot of money in these past weeks and I'm going to buy a new house for my mum, and Dorothy, they deserve it. Dennis you are due some leave? Why don't you come to England?"

Dennis sighed, "I don't have a house, or close relatives, only a few old friends, and I've lost contact with them."

"Stay with us in Portsmouth and Liverpool — we would like to have you and I'm sure my mum would like you," Robert said with a wink.

A few weeks passed and Dennis was saying goodbye to Johnson. He looked smart and Johnson told him so. "Yes, but will Mrs. Partridge like me?"

Part 3 Port Harcourt

Robert had been working for about a month in Portsmouth; Dennis had visited and had gone off to Liverpool with Dorothy. Robert saw Dennis as a kind of second father and the way Dorothy enjoyed his company, Dennis was almost a second father-in-law.

The workers had been full of questions when Robert first returned from Lagos but now things had settled down, and only John seemed to resent his return. Anne had asked a few questions when he returned but seemed not too interested in what he had to say. Bill was more interested in life in Lagos and had confessed that if he had been offered the job in Lagos he would have been sorely tempted. Robert tried to be diplomatic when he explained that Lagos was the place for a young expatriate, even Dennis was too old.

A few weeks went by and then Robert received instructions to catch a train to London and then get an underground train to Stepney Green. He should try to be at the Black Horse pub at noon and wait to be contacted by a man named Kelvin. "Well, this is a new approach. Now the serious stuff starts," Robert said to himself when he received the phone call.

Arriving at Stepney Green he found the Black Horse close to the station. Entering the pub and walking to the bar Robert ordered a pint of light beer and sat down. He wanted to make sure he was totally aware of what was said and he thought he might have to wait and have another beer before Kelvin showed up. He restrained his curiosity and just stared at the bar instead of examining the pub patrons. The bar was not crowded and there were plenty of free tables but then, it was only just before noon. Robert was deep in thought when a man came to the bar and said, "Hello Robert, I'm Kelvin. We used to go to the same school." Robert's frown became a smile as he thought to himself that no one at his school had ever spoken with that accent. Kelvin suggested they find a table and discuss old times, so they proceeded to a corner table. "Just make sure no one overhears us and nod agreement a few times. Don't ask many questions but make a comment or two as the conversation progresses."

Robert was smiling to himself, imagining someone from his school talking about a conversation "progressing".

Kelvin hunched over his drink and started to brief Robert. "When you get to Port Harcourt spend your time after work in the Port Harcourt Club where you'll be contacted by one of our operatives. The club compound was originally owned by a Greek family but they backed Biafra in the war so it was confiscated after the war. The Nigerian Government set up the club for expatriates so they could keep an eye on them and get the local gossip. Some of the staff work for the security service so be careful what you say. Our operative will introduce himself as a distant relative. Let him give you instructions, and don't ask questions." Robert wanted to ask lots of questions but he had learnt to keep them to himself. The word "operative" again sounded a bit ominous but then meeting in the Black Horse was a bit ominous in itself.

"When you return from Port Harcourt to Lagos, you'll leave for England within two days, and if anyone asks why the speedy departure say that you are required for a difficult job in Portsmouth."

Kelvin finished his drink and wished Robert goodbye. "I hope to see you at one of the school reunions."

Robert smiled and wanted to say that any of his school reunions would be a success if it was held in Liverpool jail. Robert slowly finished his beer and later caught the train to Portsmouth. At home he called Dorothy and told her he would have to go back to Nigeria for a couple of weeks and that she should either spend some time in Liverpool or come back to Portsmouth whichever she pleased. Dorothy seemed quite content to stay in Liverpool and said Dennis and his mom were having a good time. Dorothy was trying to absorb as much local culture as Liverpool had to offer and she was really interested in the history of the city. She was going to use her new computer skills to write some stories about the port area, Dennis had supplied some little tit-bits about the area that she didn't know.

In the factory there was a lot of gossip centred mainly about John who had just replaced Dennis, who had resigned. John had contacted some of his workmates and by all accounts he hated everything from the first minute he landed in Lagos. Anne smiled as she told Robert the latest news from Lagos. Jide and John were immediately at logger heads and John was already asking when he could come home. The job was only a temporary until the company could find a permanent replacement for Dennis. Robert was smiling at the thought of John interacting with Jide. He was also thinking of how John would interact with the workers.

One day Anne called Robert to the office. "You'll spend a few days in Lagos before going to Port Harcourt. Help John if you can. In Port Harcourt you should take a look at our factory, it's little more than a warehouse where we ship in pumps and other parts and there is a small operation fixing pumps if they can be fixed. There is a bit of pilfering going on and there are continual requests for tools, see if you can sort it out."

The second visa was obtained much more quickly than the first and Robert was on his way to Lagos within two weeks. On arrival only the driver met Robert at the airport and they went straight to the factory. There he met John who even seemed pleased to see him. John spilled out a litany of gripes, mostly about Jide and the workforce, but also about Nigeria in general. Robert listened and then started to tell John how to cope with the situation. It was only temporary so John could look forward to going home. John had to learn to talk to the workers; he should start by learning their names, find out about their families. Talk about education if they have kids, tell them their son might go to university and learn new skills but remind them they have skills, they can use tools and fix things. With Jide, Robert advised that John just let him do his own thing, and try not to bother him too much and to ignore his fiddles.

When Robert finally got into the factory, he was greeted by lots of handshakes and smiles, and the place was abuzz with laughter and joy. John was a bit taken aback by the reception but he was trying to remember what Robert had told him. Jide finally showed up and tried to mix with the workers but they only wanted Robert. Finally, after about thirty minutes Jide made some excuse and slunk back to his office. Robert and John left work early and were driven back to Ikeja. When they entered the compound, Johnson was ecstatic.

Johnson prepared a good meal and on the table were two large bottles of Gulder beer. John drank his beer quite swiftly but Robert struggled to finish his beer. "This Nigerian beer is dynamite. I can't handle more than one."

John replied, "Beer is one of the few things I enjoy about Nigeria." Robert excused himself and said he was tired and needed an early night.

The next few days were fun, Robert was helping the workers and John was talking to them. John found that the first thing to do was to greet a worker and then ask about his family — that broke the ice and instructions about work came last. Robert showed the repair team a few of the tricks he had learned in Portsmouth. He went out with a team to one of the ships in the harbour to fix a broken pump. The captain, who was a Dane, was surprised to see this Englishman working alongside the Nigerians and was delighted the job was fixed quickly. Robert was invited to the captain's cabin for a drink but he politely declined saying he didn't drink, but if the captain could spare a can of beer each for the men, they would surely not pass up the gift. The men were delighted and Robert advised the leader of the gang that if they did a good quick job, they might get rewards in future.

Robert booked his flight to Port Harcourt and waded through the throng at Lagos Airport. When he finally got on the tarmac, he found there were only twelve passengers, the crowd outside had been touts trying to sell bogus tickets or offering to carry bags. He sat next to a German who was on his way to the oil rigs; he worked two months on and one month off and went back to Germany every leave. The German seemed to know nothing about Port Harcourt and almost nothing about Nigeria. His philosophy seemed to be: earn as much as possible and get out as often as possible. Robert thought the German was missing so much. Finally, when they landed, they bade each other goodbye and entered the customs hall. Robert was glad to leave his new companion and this time Robert had his passport handy and everything went smoothly.

The driver took Robert to the Port Harcourt Club where he had a room booked. The room was sparse but the sheets were clean and the adjoining toilet had scented toilet paper. Robert's first thought to hope that the smell was an insecticide to keep the mossies away. On his first visit to Port Harcourt, he had stayed in a local hotel which had supplied him with two mosquito coils. His room in the club had an insecticide spray and mosquito netting around the bed. Robert was well aware that cerebral malaria was prevalent in this area, and the last thing he wanted was to get sick.

The club was a good place to stay as it was central and close to the warehouse. He could sit in the club for long periods without anyone asking why he was there, after all, he looked a bit Nigerian, or so he thought. He soon found out that most of the members were Nigerians, and he was not one of them. They seemed to be different than Lagotians.

Sitting at the bar on the second day he was approached by a tall slim Nigerian who introduced himself as Felix. Felix said that they might be related and would Robert like to sit outside and discuss the family. Outside was hot and sticky but Felix explained that they would not be disturbed and most of the bar staff were in the pay of the Nigerian Security Organisation. Robert now realised that this was the operative. Felix was an Ibo and any family relationship was very improbable but that ruse had gotten them to a place where they would not be overheard. Felix explained that they were to do a "job" — one that needed some preparation, and firstly they were going to take a fishing trip. On the Saturday they would meet at the wharf and go fishing. In the meantime, Robert should get on with his job at the warehouse and maybe try to see a few relatives. Felix even told him the village where they lived. After a couple of drinks, they departed and Robert went back to his room. Lots of questions came to his mind but the one that stuck was why they were going fishing. He was grateful that Felix had given him his relatives' addresses. Felix must know a lot about Robert, his family and his story.

Robert met the manager of the warehouse who was really a foreman. The warehouse was a bit of a shambles with new stock mixed with old broken rubbish. Robert had to look through the junk and decide what could be fixed and what had to be thrown out. He took one of the men and while sorting the rubbish they put possibly usable parts in a bin. The worker was a bit astonished at this white man getting his hands dirty but rather enjoyed this morning's work. After it was finished Robert went to see the manager. This man knew a bit about pumps but nothing about management. Robert asked what happened to the rubbish and found it was tossed out. Then Robert enquired if the manager knew anyone who would buy scrap metal. The manager said he would ask around.

Robert then asked for a list of all the workers and when he had the list, he went into the factory to talk to the men. Robert greeted each man, asked his name, asked after his family and shook hands. There was one missing and was told he was sick, so he asked for a list of absences over the past month. It appeared that this one man was often absent so Robert seconded one of the workers who knew where he lived and they set out to visit the sick man. The worker was not at home and asking around they found he was at work on the dock where he was fixing someone's pump. They arrived at the wharf and found the absentee. Robert asked whether this was a part-time job. Seeing a workmate with Robert the man lost his tongue. Robert looked at the pump and saw that he was doing a good job. Robert asked whether he wanted to work for the company or work for himself. The man sheepishly said the company, so Robert told him to finish the pump and come back to work. Robert had to admit to himself that the man had initiative and could do a job — all he needed was to be pointed in the right direction. The worker with Robert was astonished that the man had not been sacked. This white man was a bit different.

Robert's charm offensive was working, the work was being done more efficiently, the men were showing him family photos and they listened intently when he started to tell them stories of Britain. Robert's problem was that he couldn't stop thinking about fishing. What did it mean? He couldn't wait for Friday night when he was to meet Felix in the club. He arrived at the club early and sat outside. Finally, Felix arrived. Felix explained that they were just going fishing, and that it was important that Robert should enjoy it and keep an eye out for any details that seemed out of the ordinary. Robert laughed internally thinking that almost everything in Nigeria was out of the ordinary. Felix asked if Robert had ever been fishing and as the reply was in the negative Felix said he would learn something new. They were to meet at the harbour, where the small boats were berthed, at eight in the morning. As the boat's owner spoke some English Robert should be careful what he said. After a couple of beers Felix left and Robert went to his room to have a fitful sleep, with lots of fishing in his dreams. He was awake before dawn and could hardly wait for the sun to rise.

At eight the next morning Robert was on the dock and Felix introduced him to the captain and then they went fishing. Robert was a quick learner and soon mastered fishing, Nigerian style. They had very crude rods and mainly had line and hooks trailing off the back and side of the boat. While getting to the fishing site Robert tried to take in as much information about the river banks as he could but obviously missed a few important anomalies. While they were fishing Felix quietly asked Robert whether he had seen a man with binoculars on one of the banks. Robert admitted he missed that one. Robert didn't also notice a small fishing boat that tailed them until they stopped to start fishing. Felix explained that they were being watched so they just had to fish, catch fish, and go back to the dock. They did catch plenty of fish and Robert was thinking that his fishing trip would be a good story to tell Dorothy.

The better fish were put in buckets and baths and kept alive until they landed. Felix had a couple of containers filled with ice in which he put some of the better fish which he sent to the warehouse. The rest he gave to the captain and some of the dock hands explaining that the white man enjoyed the fishing and wanted to share his luck. They were a bit dumbstruck, he had paid for the trip and was now giving away most of the catch, Felix explained to them that Robert it was just sport-crazy English!

On Sunday morning Robert contacted the manager and told him to contact the workers to bring their families to the warehouse and enjoy a fish barbecue. Robert then set out to get some beer, soft drinks, bread, tomatoes and onions, with the help of a driver, who was very enthusiastic. The workers gathered and the fish were presented to them and they were told to cook the fish the way they wanted. Robert got to meet the families and told everyone to be friends as they were one big family. He made more adoring friends in one afternoon than he could have imagined. This was a very successful barbecue. He was a little disappointed that Felix was not there. Felix had paid for the fishing he had organised everything and now Robert was getting all the praise. Where did Felix go? Where was he now?

On Monday Robert decided to sort out the tool problem. The men loved him so much he could have done almost anything and they would have agreed. He told them at the end of the work day they were to hand in all their tools and he would have each tool engraved with name of the owner and then they would get those tools back and they were theirs. He decided on a basic tool kit for each man and wanted to get a tool box for each set of tools, but found they were not available in the market so he ordered them from Lagos. He worked into the night to engrave the tools and had to get a taxi to the club. The taxi driver spoke some English and as they chatted Robert came to know that the distribution of fish was well known in the town. Robert started to realise how visible he was in this community, no matter what his skin colour, he was an eccentric white man. The taxi driver wanted to know if he was going fishing again. One of the bar men in the club also wanted to know the same thing. He explained to the barman that he had not been fishing in Nigeria before and loved the experience. Later he thought maybe he should not have talked to the barman but he had said nothing out of the ordinary.

His next task was to visit the village where his relatives lived. The driver took him about twenty miles outside of Port Harcourt to the edge of the village but declined to drive into the village. Robert wondered about that but walked about five hundred yards into the village centre. He saw some men playing cards and walked up and introduced himself as Robert Partridge. The game stopped but no one smiled and one man stood up. Robert sensed that he was not in a friendly place and wondered whether he had come to the right village. The man standing introduced himself as the brother of the sister who had married Robert's father. Robert was taken aback that his father had another wife. This man started to tell of the problem Robert's father had caused. There had been a marriage producing a child and then the father had left; gone to sea. His sister had never received any money and had to bring up her son on her own, the family were very unhappy and wanted compensation.

Robert asked if he could see his 'second' mother but that was declined. Robert was now in a delicate situation so he said he would try to find his father and make everything right. He bid them good day and beat a fairly hastily retreat to the car. The driver explained that this was not a good village and that he would not drive closer. Robert realised that this village had revealed a few difficult truths and had presented him with lots of problems such as how to tell his mother. This was a very different reception to the one he had during his first visit to Port Harcourt. Maybe the distant relatives were friendlier than the close ones. Another mother and a half brother or sister, he had not thought to ask about; this had all taken him by surprise and might need a little delicacy when he told his mother.

Robert had sorted out the warehouse and the workers but his personal life was in turmoil. A second mother, a father at sea with maybe other wives and children. How was he going to find out the truth and then how was he going to tell his mother? It dawned on him that he was working for an organisation that could come up with those answers, and that it just needed the right time to ask the questions. He was now so wrapped up with Felix and fishing he couldn't wait for next Saturday and the second fishing trip.

Saturday morning rolled around and Robert was eager to get on the boat. Felix again warned him about saying very much about anything except maybe work. Felix also impressed on him the need to be observant but not to stare at anything for a long time. Robert didn't see anything unusual and there was no man with binoculars. This time the fishing was better and they soon filled the buckets and started back to the wharf. On the way back Felix was in a very long conversation with the captain, they were speaking a sort of Pidgin so Robert couldn't understand much except it all seemed to be about the boat. When they pulled into the wharf there was a much bigger crowd than last time and a lot of jostling to get some of the fish — free fish! Felix travelled with Robert to deposit the fish for the next day's barbecue and when they were alone Felix explained to Robert, that the following Saturday they would be going night fishing alone. The captain didn't go out at night but Felix had persuaded him to let them take the boat out alone. The captain had been persuaded with more money and the fact that this was the last weekend for Robert in Port Harcourt and that this white man had never tried night fishing. Robert was not too happy about night fishing but he trusted Felix and realised something important was to happen.

The Sunday barbecue was a great success and there seemed to be lots more people than Robert expected including a band. Everybody was so happy it took Robert's mind away from the next weekend. In the week he had to make sure everything he had put in place carried on when he left. He was due to fly out on the Sunday evening so he would not get to enjoy the party and that meant the manager would be left in charge. He impressed on the manager that his job and that of the workers would only be guaranteed if the work practices he had initiated were continued. He talked to each worker telling them about their skills and giving them advice about how to bring up their children and how to make sure they could all read and write. The workers just lapped it up and would sit around during their breaks talking positively about Robert. The tool boxes finally arrived and that day there was great rejoicing. Now Robert was set for the adventure on Saturday. Robert laughed to himself he had no children and was telling the workers how to bring up children.

Saturday arrived and Robert had to kill time until the late afternoon so he spent some time in the club. He chatted with a few expatriates but couldn't wait till four in the afternoon when he would go to the harbour. Felix was already there when Robert arrived and with a few well-wishers (probably waiting for more fish) waving them goodbye, they pulled away and headed down towards the estuary. Robert did notice a few faces he had seen before but no one with binoculars. As it grew dark — sunset was very swift and in about twenty minutes it went from sunset to almost complete darkness — Felix guided the boat off the main channel into a smaller channel. Felix then stopped the motor and they drifted towards a dilapidated jetty where they anchored. It became almost completely dark and they then moved to the jetty. Felix asked Robert to hold the rope so that the boat was steady and Felix hoisted himself on to the jetty. From the boat Robert made out a figure approaching, it seemed to be a small man in a suit carrying a briefcase. Felix lowered the man into the boat and then jumped on board pushing the boat away from the jetty. Felix found an oar and started to paddle the boat into the middle of the stream. Meanwhile the little man made his way to the back of the boat without word to Robert. Robert tried to help Felix but he was motioned to take care of the steering. After a short while Felix started the motor and they made their way to the main channel. They moved quite swiftly out towards the sea and the boat started to feel the swell, Felix was using a compass and said nothing. The passenger was equally quiet. Robert was just wondering if he was going to be sea sick.

In the distance there was a light and as they approached there was the dim outline of a large ship appearing. They pulled alongside and were greeted from above by what sounded like a Scottish accent. Felix answered and a rope descended from above. Robert was asked to hold the rope tight and to make sure he was also holding on to the boat. A large basket was lowered and Felix helped the little man climb aboard. The little Nigerian was lifted up and Robert's thought was that they had never spoken a word to each other. Once the little man was aboard Robert was told to release the rope and they moved away from the ship. Robert was thankful that the sea was so calm or he might have been hanging on the rope over the ocean.

Felix quickly took charge and they motored towards the estuary and once inside Felix said they should fish. The fishing was not too good so they moved further along the river and came close to the right-hand shore. They then stopped and did some more fishing. This time the fish were biting better and they started to fill the buckets. Robert was feeling sleepy and so Felix told him to lie down and have a nap. Robert must have slept a good while because he awoke to see dawn. Robert wondered if Felix had slept. Felix explained they should do a little more fishing and get back to the wharf at about eight. As they approached the dock, they could see the captain waiting anxiously. It was all smiles as they docked, and lots of "well-wishers" were waiting for their fish. Robert told the captain that night fishing was an experience he wanted but it was not as good as fishing during the day. The captain was pleased and he nodded his head at the Englishman's realisation of what he knew already.

The barbecue party was in full swing when Robert said goodbye to go to the airport. The driver wanted to get back to the party but Robert made him wait. It was a wise move as the plane to Lagos was cancelled.

Robert had to go back to the club and book a room for another night. The driver was anxious to get back to the party and so Robert let him go with instructions to pick him up in the morning to go to the airport. Lying on the bed Robert reviewed all that had happened that day. Who was the little Nigerian with the briefcase and what was in the case? Where was Felix? He had disappeared more or less as soon as they had landed. As he lay there he started to sweat and realised he had forgotten to put on the air conditioner. The cool air had immediately induced sleep and the next thing he knew it was light.

The Monday morning flight was not cancelled but was nearly full with passengers from the previous day. Robert half expected to see Felix but he didn't show up. The flight to Lagos was uneventful and he decided to go straight to the house in Ikeja. Johnson was there and was so happy to see him and made one or two complaints about John. Robert relaxed and thought about his flight to the UK and seeing Dorothy again. It was the first time he had relaxed in the past three weeks and he dropped off to sleep in the chair. He was awoken by John with the news that a replacement had been found and John was going home in a few weeks. Robert's mind was elsewhere but he said he was happy for John. Robert wondered whether he would like John's job again, he could handle Lagos, the job and Jide. Their evening was spent at the Ikeja Country Club with John in very good spirits and Robert enjoying a couple of Star beers. John was pleased that work was easier but he couldn't wait till he arrived in England.

The next morning Robert was to fly out and declined a trip to the factory. John told him that the workers would be disappointed but Robert gave the excuse he was tired. He was really wanting to get home to see Dorothy and his mother, and he was also conscious that he should say very little about Port Harcourt. Later that morning John came back with the driver and they went to the airport. Everything went smoothly and Robert said goodbye to Nigeria. He felt he would never return. The flight was uneventful but all Robert could think about was a small man with a briefcase, and Felix.

At Gatwick he was met by the same driver who had first met him when he had come for the interview from Manchester. He was taken to a block of flats and told to go to number 9. When he entered the flat it looked familiar. He was ushered into the office and and was confronted by two men, both in identical dark brown suits with purple ties. Of course he immediately recognised them; this time they took it in turns speaking. They thanked him for a job well done and said that he should go back to Portsmouth and resume his job but to be prepared to move again. He was to tell Dorothy very little about his time in Port Harcourt, and also he should tell his mother very little except about his trip to the relatives. Robert wondered how they knew about his relatives. Finally, they asked if he had any questions.

"Where is Felix"?

That bought a weak smile to both their faces and the one on the left spoke. "Felix is one of our best operatives but one of the most independent. He could be anywhere from Ghana to Cameroon and he will let us know when he has a new project. He might even be looking for your father." That last phrase was such a surprise that Robert couldn't think of any more questions.

The driver dropped him at the train station and he was on his way to Liverpool. He was greeted at the station by Dorothy, his mother and Dennis and they all enjoyed the moment. Dorothy couldn't wait to show him her computer and some of her stories. His mother didn't seem too upset with the second wife, and anyhow she was getting a divorce for desertion. Dennis enjoyed the news about Lagos, Johnson and John. Dennis had a job fixing motors and was loving living with Robert's mom. It was like a role reversal — Robert was used to telling the stories and now he was the listener; in a way he was glad because he was not sure how much he could say.

Dorothy and Robert caught the train to Portsmouth with only one piece of important luggage, Dorothy's computer. Robert went back to work and Dorothy was happy to spend her time writing stories. The workers were all eager to hear about life in Lagos and how John was fairing. Apparently, the gossip was that John was to come home soon as a replacement had been found. Robert already knew that news but he showed surprise when the workers told him. Anne didn't ask any questions but intimated that Robert might get a call soon and should be prepared to move at a moment's notice. Robert marvelled at how Anne always seemed to be one jump ahead. Anne was also happy about their warehouse in Port Harcourt it seemed to be working properly.

Robert got a call from London to say that he should meet a Mr. Smith at Portsmouth train station the next day. There was no other information about this visit and Robert was thinking it might be another assignment. On his way to the train station Robert was wondering he would recognise Mr. Smith. It turned out that Mr. Smith recognised Robert. They went to a hotel where Mr. Smith booked a room and they adjourned to the lounge. Robert learned that the Nigerian Security Organisation had suspicions about Robert and that they would be looking for him. Robert was to go home, collect his wife and some belongings and come back to the hotel where a room was booked for them.

"What about work?"

"Anne will know and have your letter of resignation prepared, your personal belonging will be gathered and ready for when you leave for Canada."

Robert went home and told Dorothy to pack some clothes and that it was possible they may not come back. The computer was top priority for Dorothy so it was put it in a separate suitcase. At the hotel Mr. Smith checked them into a room and took them to dinner and answered a few questions. Robert was in a bit of shock but Dorothy started with the questions.

"When are we going to Canada, will I be able to take my computer?"

Robert was thinking that computer had become like her right arm and he was a little bit jealous. Robert now started to ask a few serious questions. Why was the Nigerian Security Organisation so interested in them? What was so important? Dorothy was a little perplexed as Robert had told her very little about Port Harcourt. Mr. Smith informed them that the little Nigerian they had spirited away was a top accountant for a Nigerian oil company and his briefcase was full of financial details that would be useful to the British Government. Robert asked why he had been needed on the operation and asked whether it was not an expensive way to get information.

"Our organisation has the main job of collecting information; you were there to assure the accountant that he was not being kidnapped by some Nigerian group. You have cost us very little in comparison with other operations. You have been trained in another profession and have shown you are a leader and a quick learner, in any other organisation we would have claimed an education rebate," Mr. Smith said with a laugh.

Robert and Dorothy were told not to phone their relatives and if they wished they could write letters saying they were taking an extended holiday. These letters were to be handed to the driver who would pick them up from the hotel. They were to leave the envelopes open so that a picture postcard could be inserted from wherever the letters were sent. They were to stay in the hotel and not go out. Everything was paid for and they should not touch their bank accounts or use credit cards. They would be given some money before they left the UK and the driver would have their passports and tickets, and they would not be flying from Heathrow. They would be met in Canada and everything would be arranged, even a job for Robert. Mr. Smith said that the Nigerian Security Organisation (NSO) might lose interest after a while as they already knew what was missing (and where it was) but they wanted to know how the accountant was spirited away.

"Enjoy Canada and if you meet any Nigerians, be careful," was his statement as they were finishing dinner.

Robert asked one final question: "If they are after me then they must be after Felix. Are you taking care of him?"

"Felix is looking after Felix, he is a very independent operator, and in our section, is known as a legend."

Stranded

Mary hated Lagos, she hated the people, the climate, the club, and she hated everything but her husband, George. Even he came in for a rough time for bringing her to this "god-forsaken hole". The flight to Lagos was difficult and George relished the expectation that this job was going to be a challenge.

George was the chief engineer for a company in Ikeja on the outskirts of Lagos. He was good at his job and was liked by everyone; he had worked abroad before but this was the first time in Africa. Mary had always refused to live in England without him but according to her this was the worst place in which she had been forced to live. George jokingly told his friends that Mary didn't trust him to live alone as he might pick up some local bird. Many of his friends thought that would be preferable to living with Mary; she had alienated all of them with her attitude to almost anything. George had often told his friends that women can be hard and he had one of the hardest; they agreed without hesitation.

George and Mary had come to Nigeria in 1978 for his first time tour of ten months with two months leave at the end of the tour. He was given a large house in the GRA (Government Residential Area) which was owned by the company's owner. Apparently, the company paid a high rent for the house and it was one of the best in the area. The other free perks were a car with a driver, a houseboy, a gardener and a guard. The house had several air-conditioned rooms and a generator in case of power cuts (which were quite frequent). The house was well decorated and was the envy of his new friends. Even Mary was impressed with the house but unimpressed with everything else and she let George know at every opportunity.

George's job was not too demanding but he was technically on call twenty-four hours a day. As the telephones were unreliable a messenger was sent if he was needed to supervise the repair of a breakdown. Normally he worked from nine to four but he quickly joined the Lagos Country Club and started to have a few drinks and a game of snooker on his way home. Mary assumed that he worked till six and George never let her think otherwise. George loved his snooker and soon became a popular figure in the air-conditioned snooker room. He often played with the Nigerian members and they always liked a small bet on each game. This was an added attraction for George and he could well afford to lose many games without any dent in his pocket. One particular Nigerian member, Soji, was his favourite opponent as they were pretty equal in ability. Soji was from an influential Lagotian family and spoke impeccable English; he had been a pilot in England towards the end of the war and had married a Scottish girl. Soji was a straightforward guy and would often frown when he heard expats speak Pidgin English with Nigerians. He had a job at the airport helping to train pilots and overseeing the air traffic controllers. Although George was fairly new to the club, Soji picked him out as an expat who he could call a friend. Soji had a low opinion of most of the expats in the club and a similar opinion of most of his fellow countrymen.

Soji would bring his wife to the club on a Wednesday evening to watch the film and he suggested that George could bring his wife and while they were watching the film, he and George could play snooker. Mary was not too enthusiastic about going to the club but George pointed out that she was miserable in the house every day, and that a change might be good for her. Mary couldn't deny that she was housebound, maybe it was a good idea. She had been to the club on the occasional Saturday afternoon and anyone who listened to her horror stories was in for a bad time.

The first meeting of Soji, Helen, George and Mary, was a bit frosty at first but for Mary, meeting another female Brit meant she could tell about her frustrations with Nigeria. Helen had to bear the horror stories Mary would tell: the servants were stealing, the gardener was useless, the guard slept all night and the driver was a maniac. After the first evening Helen was reluctant to meet Mary again but Soji persuaded her that Mary had gotten a lot off her chest and maybe the second time would be easier. He was wrong but Helen was now better able to cope with the complaints and anyway it was a better film.

At the second meeting Helen had been sitting with a group of ladies when Mary arrived; it would mean she was not alone. Among the ladies were two Nigerians but that didn't stop Mary. She told them that she would lock the pantry and only take out the food needed; she even counted the sugar cubes. The first houseboy left within a month and the second houseboy had been sacked after one week; he had kept looking at her. Mary was good looking with an attractive figure and long blonde hair but one of the ladies pointed out that maybe the houseboy had been waiting for instructions. Mary was a fast talker when excited and it was possible the boy couldn't properly understand her but Mary dismissed that possibility. The gardener had been asked to plant some flowers and do weeding; his work was not satisfactory to Mary. The gardener was trying to explain what he was doing when she hit him and knocked him down. She told this story with relish but most of the women were shocked and said she was lucky he had not hit her back. To the relief of the women, it was time to see the movie before Mary told them any more horror stories. Helen had to sit next to Mary during the movie but Mary shut up as it was a good movie.

George was warned by some expats that there would be trouble if she didn't control herself. He had tried to explain to Mary that she was dealing with other human beings and she should not throw stones at the guard even if he was sleeping, and certainly not punch the driver if he had a near miss. She did try for a while but she hated everything about Nigeria and couldn't help falling into her old ways. Mary left the GRA very occasionally but on the few occasions when George took her into Lagos, he had to withstand a torrent of complaints. She was horrified by the open sewers and the smells, found the crowds and the heat oppressive, she even hated the beach. Much to Helen's relief George only bought Mary to the club infrequently but he still came for snooker on Wednesday nights, often staying to near midnight.

As the first tour of duty was coming to an end, Mary could only talk about getting back to civilisation. She seemed to be coming to the club more often and the regulars were counting the days to her departure. George was not so happy about his fast-approaching long leave. He liked his job, loved Nigeria and even liked the hot humid weather; he was not your average expat. He confided in Soji that he found England boring and he would spend most of his time visiting relatives and friends and telling them stories they would not believe. In turn they would bore him with their day-to-day problems and their parochial outlook on everything. He would drink weak warm English beer and long for a cold Star or Gulder. Soji thought of England as his second home and wished he were going instead of George, but of course not with Mary. Soji had spent a good time in London and would love to see a play.

Helen longed to go to the UK, she envied Mary's escape for two months but looked forward to the escape from Mary for two months.

Two months passed very quickly for everyone except George; all the time Mary had nagged him to resign. George had been in a bad mood after one week in England and had only cheered up in the last week with the thought of returning to Lagos. George was bored and had spent a lot of time in the local pub to be away from Mary. He had tried to persuade Mary to stay in England but even though she hated Lagos she would not let George go alone.

The flight back to Lagos was a disaster which even George had not enjoyed. He had decided to fly Nigerian Airways. There were numerous delays, a near riot in Heathrow and two of the three suitcases had not arrived in Lagos. Mary was livid, she had repeatedly told him they should fly British Caledonian or any European airline but George was obstinate and decided on Nigerian Airways. Even flying business class, the flight was not comfortable and the food was only just edible. George had tried to ignore all her complaints but he was not superman. A driver picked them up at the airport and to Mary's total displeasure George told him to stop at the club before going home. Mary had protested and George had frightened her into submission. His face seemed full of hatred, his blue eyes were cold and she had never felt them pierce through her before. George had half raised his hand before he told her to shut up.

He didn't hit her but a few drops of spit from the *shh* had landed on her face. Inside she was trembling and this was the first time she had felt afraid of George so she did shut up.

Arriving at the club George jumped out of the car and almost ran inside to the bar. Mary slowly followed; she wanted to go home and cry as George had never before intimidated her. In a curious way she wanted to see what would happen when she sat beside him in the bar. She hated the bar but she had to reason with George, this had been a tiring trip for both of them and maybe George needed to unwind. By the time she sat down George had almost finished his first bottle of Star and was ordering the second; he didn't offer her a drink. The second bottle was finished almost as quickly as the first and a third bottle was ordered. George was now starting to giggle and was talking very loudly to everyone but Mary. She ordered a drink and asked him to pay, George looked her with cold blue eyes and said "Piss off." Mary turned white and tears glistened in her eyes, she searched in her hand bag for Nigerian money. Searching her hand bag was a defence mechanism she was trying to hold back the tears.

The barman quickly came to the rescue and said, "Next time, madam." Now she was lost and didn't know what to do so she slowly sipped her drink while she thought out her next move.

Meanwhile, George was talking to a stranger at the bar and totally ignoring her. She finished her drink and decided to take action. George felt a tug on his sleeve which he ignored then there was a stronger tug that made him mad. He turned to Mary and looked her straight in the eyes and said nothing, but the look made her recoil. George had never hit her before but she was expecting a first. George spoke slowly but calmly: "Go to the house, unpack the luggage such as it is and send the driver back for me. Don't wait up." It was all said so slowly and precisely she couldn't question the instructions so she slowly backed out of the bar and went to the car.

George came home drunk late that night and fell asleep on the couch. He was still asleep at ten in the morning and the servants were instructed not to enter the lounge. At half past ten George woke up without a hangover and in a good mood, he was looking forward to a day at work. Mary bought him a cup of coffee half expecting a problem but not a smile and a peck on the cheek. Now she was confused and George was anxious to get to work; she was anxious for him to leave so she could have a good cry.

The next few weeks were very peaceful and even Helen said that the vacation had calmed Mary down. George was a little infatuated with Helen, she was so calm and easy going and she liked Soji to enjoy himself. She worked part-time in Lagos as a secretary to the managing director of an oil company and yet with all that travelling, she never seemed to be upset or frustrated. George thought Soji was lucky to have such a wife. Even Soji had remarked to George that Mary had changed somewhat; which was unusual for Soji who never made personal statements. But Soji was no ordinary Nigerian. He and Helen had heard about the incident in the bar but had put it down to a long flight making their friends irritable.

Several weeks passed before Mary went back to her old complaining ways. George had calmed down and everyone noticed his snooker games went on much later than six in the evening. Helen was generally the one to put a stop to the Wednesday snooker games going past midnight, Mary was still a little afraid of voicing her opinion on that matter. Helen found Mary quieter and easier to talk to but Mary was again starting to become more difficult.

George initially had many problems at work to solve but then work seemed to settle into a dull routine. He often left work early and headed for the club. One day the managing director asked George if he would go to Enugu to an associated company to fix one of their problems. George was over the moon and agreed immediately, he loved a challenge.

His first trip to eastern Nigeria was for one week, he was then back in Lagos for one week and then back to Enugu for another week. Mary was irritated by his absence but it gave her a chance to abuse the servants. She had the car and driver while he was away, but there was nowhere to go. She could go to the market but she hated it and sent the house girl to buy vegetables and fruit. There was one store in Ikeja run by Arabs that occasionally had some imported food and then there was the club. She was bored; having read all the books bought back from England, played a lot of Solitaire and tried painting with no success. The club had a library, not up to Mary's standards, but she would often let the driver take her to the club so she could get new books. If she went early in the morning the club would be almost deserted but later in the afternoon there might be a few ladies she could entertain with her complaints. Female members of the club started to dread Mary's arrival; those picking up their children from the school next door couldn't really avoid her. The women who disliked her most were the European women married to Nigerians. George was as popular as ever but he was starting to get warnings about his wife's behaviour. He was even warned by one of the women that he was giving her too much free time in the club and maybe some lonely male member might take an interest. In a community with a shortage of females George could have been inviting problems, but Mary's reputation was a big warning sign.

Things came to a head one Wednesday night when George had left the snooker room early and heard Mary haranguing a group of ladies. He pulled Mary aside and told her to go home and send the driver back for him. She saw that look in his face that scared her so she obeyed.

George came home late that night and slept in the spare bedroom. In the morning when Mary arose, he had already gone to work. Later that night when he came home Mary tried to talk to him but he was very abusive and so she retreated. During the next few weeks their relationship was very frosty and they rarely talked; he always slept in the spare bedroom when he was home, and he was spending more and more time in Enugu. George had also lost two suitcases on his travels and Mary wanted to tell him to claim off the insurance but she was too scared.

It was approaching the end of his second tour and Mary was hoping to get back to England and persuade George to resign. She was so looking forward to going back home, and the thought was fortifying her in her loneliness.

One day George left for the east and that was the last time she saw him. He had given her plenty of money for house-keeping but had not really said good bye or given any indication he would not be back.

After two weeks the driver stopped coming with the car. The managing director came and informed Mary she should vacate the house within one week; he had assumed she had left Nigeria as her airfare had been paid to George. Mary was in a state of shock, "There must be a mistake, George is in Enugu on company business."

"George resigned two months ago and arranged to take one month's leave. The driver was supplied for an extra two weeks so that you could pack and leave," the managing director explained. Mary didn't believe him and said so in very impolite terms. The manager took a deep breath and reiterated that the house should be vacated in one week otherwise she would be forcibly removed. He added that he was giving her much more time than she had given her second houseboy, his nephew. "I can do no more for you even if I thought you deserved my help," and with those words the managing director turned and left, only adding that the guard would remain to protect the house but that the rest of the servants were needed elsewhere.

Mary was not convinced George had left her so she went to the bedroom to check his wardrobe. There were a few shirts and a pair of trousers she had bought him in England and little else. She went to the spare room but there was nothing there. She opened the locked desk and found her passport with the horrible photo but George's passport was missing. She then noticed most of George's possessions were missing, his mother's photo which was on a table on his side of the bed was missing, she had not noticed its absence. In the bathroom she found his dressing gown on the back of the door. She had bought that gown in Singapore several years ago; she held it to her face, smelt it and carefully took it down. The smell of George was on the gown and that bought back many happy memories. She pulled out a suitcase and packed away George's things all the while saying to herself that George would need them when he returned from the east.

After packing George's things, she started to pack her own and realised she didn't have enough suitcases, George had lost at least three. It was then she realised that George had planned his disappearance. Now she started to think about her own predicament; who would help her? It was Wednesday so she decided to go to the club to talk to Helen and Soji. She would have to get a taxi and hoped that Soji would bring her home. The GRA at night was a scary place even though most of the houses were heavily guarded; with no husband to protect her she was vulnerable. Suddenly she had an urge to get out of the house it seemed so stuffy even though the air conditioning was keeping it cool. She was continually looking for marks of George's presence and finding none she had to get out into the fresh air.

As she walked out of the house to find a taxi, she realised how hot and humid it was and she started to regret leaving the house. She should have bought her swimming costume but she couldn't return to the house although she would have to return at some point — that could be faced later. The drive in the taxi was over very quickly and she paid the fare without objection, she had never learnt to haggle. The club was almost deserted as it was well before lunch. She picked up an old newspaper and cursed herself for not bringing a book to read. The staff were cleaning up from the night before and making a poor job of it. Mary wanted to get up and show them how to do it properly but she restrained herself. She started to think about how she treated the servants poorly and that houseboy staring at her, if only she had known it was the managing director's nephew. The young man had been scared of her and almost ran when she ordered him out of the house. At the time she had enjoyed it but now she felt ashamed of herself. Now she was being ordered out of the house by his uncle. Mary was feeling weak and vulnerable and she started to blame George — who else could she blame?

The head barman had been told by the gateboy that the madam had arrived in a taxi and not with the normal driver and so he sensed something was wrong. He came over to Mary and asked if there was a problem. She was quick to give him a negative reply but she would have loved to blurt out the whole sorry story. She realised that her problems were showing on her face so she went to the toilet to check it out. In the mirror she looked normal, her eyes were not even red, so she thought the barman might have a sixth sense.

A few men came in for lunch but it was nearly three o'clock before the first woman arrived. She had met Sally before and under normal circumstances would have tried to avoid her. Sally was a down-to-earth Mancunian married to a Nigerian. She, too, often complained about Nigeria but got on well with Nigerians. Sally was almost the opposite of her husband, Wole. He was quiet, softly spoken and friendly; Sally had an indiscriminate tongue. Many

226

expats had caught the rough edge, particularly the ones she described as "up themselves". Sally thought that of Mary, but she ordered a beer and sat down opposite her. She sensed that Mary had a problem, probably because she hardly said a word. The steward bought Sally's beer and she took a swig from the bottle before pouring most of the rest into a glass. Mary shuddered and Sally looked her in the eye and said, "What's the problem?" Mary was flabbergasted. How did she know?

"Since I sat down you have looked like you wanted to say something but are holding it back, thus you have a problem."

Sally was on her second beer before Mary let out her secret, and in a way, it was a relief. Mary was staggered by Sally's summing up of the situation. "You hate Nigeria but your husband seems to like it, you badgered and bullied him so he left. I hate Nigeria and tell everyone except my husband and his relatives, he loves Nigeria and I accept that. I safeguard against him leaving me and I would never leave him. Do you have any money and do you have a house in the UK?"

Sally had come straight to the realities of Mary's problem and Mary almost zombie-like answered all the questions. The next question was the biggest shock: "Do you need money for your airfare?" Mary was loath to answer that question but admitted she had some money but nowhere near enough for an airfare. If anyone could lend her the money, she would surely pay it back.

"I'm offering you the money. I know you'll pay it back, so do you want it?"

Mary said "Yes" and burst into tears. Sally put her arms around Mary as two ladies walked into the lounge.

"I thought you preferred men," quipped a fat lady.

"Shut your foul mouth and order us a couple of beers. Mary's husband is in the east and she is missing him." Mary was relieved at how Sally said nothing about their conversation and how well she had handled the situation. Mary enjoyed the afternoon and by the time Helen and Soji arrived she was "flying" on three beers.

Soji and Helen arrived at about six and Soji went straight to the snooker room. Sally took Helen aside and told her the story, Helen was not too sympathetic. Helen liked George and didn't entirely believe Mary's story. Helen told Soji later, but he was not going to hear bad things about his friend. Mary's problem of getting home having been solved by Sally, Wole would drive Mary home or she could stay at Sally's house. Mary immediately agreed to stay with Sally and Wole as staying at her own house would bring back too many memories.

Sally's house was in a rough part of Ikeja that Mary had never visited. It was small and not air conditioned but well-furnished and well-kept. The bedroom had a ceiling fan but Mary was not used to the heat and had an uncomfortable night's sleep. The bed was comfortable but thoughts of George kept coming into

228

her mind. Had she been a good wife? Oh, to have the chance again she would surely have tried harder, with all the things he had recently done she still loved him. She seemed to wake every hour and when dawn came it was a relief.

Sally apologised that breakfast was only egg on toast but Mary enjoyed it then realised that in her freezer was plenty of food, including bacon. When she told Sally that they should raid her freezer they both had a good laugh. Wole dropped them at the house and then went to work. Sally was an organiser and a tireless worker and they went through the house deciding what Mary should take and what they could either sell or give away. Mary didn't really want to part with anything but Sally pointed out that she needed a couple more suitcases and even then, she would be overweight for an economy flight. Mary had never flown economy but now she had no choice. Sally knew plenty of poor Nigerian families who would love some of the throw-away stuff and they decided that selling things might attract too much attention.

When Wole picked them up in the late afternoon they had plenty of food and throw-away items to load into the car. Sally pointed out that she would distribute some of the items after Mary had left so as not to attract too much attention. Mary was seeing Sally in a different light — here was a smart woman who could control difficult situations and Mary wished she could be more like her. The second night's sleep was much better and the next morning Sally had arranged for Wole to take them to Lagos, to his father's house. Sally was going to the market to buy a couple of cheap, locally made suitcases and she needed to keep Mary well away from the purchasing ordeal.

Wole drove them to almost the middle of Lagos Island to his father's house. This was another part of Lagos Mary had not seen and of course it had open sewers on both sides of the street but the smell was not too bad as there had been some rain. Sally introduced Mary to her father-in-law who was delighted to see them. This little man spoke impeccable English and told Mary that Sally was his favourite woman in the world since his wife had died. Sally pointed out that he had two daughters but he still stressed she was the favourite. Mary realised this was the first time she had talked to a Nigerian as an equal and she was enjoying the experience. Ayo was his name and he had been a tailor before he semi-retired, with no pension he had to do a few jobs and relied on his children for a bit of extra cash, Olawole was always generous. He had learnt English at a Catholic school and had made all his children learn English. That was a wise move as all of his six children were doing well.

When Sally left for the market, he made a cup of tea and he sat with Mary on the veranda. The tea was followed by a beer and a good discussion about England. Mary realised that this little man seemed to know more about England, from his sons, than she did.

Sitting outside Ayo's pokey little house observing an interesting street life was enjoyable and she felt at home among friends. An old man passed as they were sitting outdoors and said something in Yoruba and Ayo replied in Yoruba. Mary asked for a translation and Ayo said the man had asked whether he had acquired a new daughter-in-law and Ayo had replied she was just a friend. This was the first time any Nigerian had called her a friend and she was so happy. Too late her eyes were opening to Nigeria and all the things she had not previously seen.

Sally came back with a couple of suitcases that Mary thought might fall apart but they lasted well and Mary still keeps them as mementoes. They sat and chatted and shared a few more beers, which Sally had acquired at the market. Ayo was unhappy to see them go when Wole came to pick them up and he gave Mary a kiss on the cheek; another first.

What a day — so many new things.

The week passed quickly and Sally was able to purchase a ticket in Naira on Nigerian Airways. Expatriates were supposed to pay in foreign currency but Sally had bullied them into accepting local currency for her "sister's" ticket. Sally came to the airport and also arranged that Mary didn't pay excess baggage. Sally explained that the suitcases of most Nigerians were almost empty on the flight to London but on the way back, they would be full to overflowing. Sally saw to all of the rest of the formalities and escorted Mary to the departure gate. Mary expected to say goodbye there but with a few Yoruba phrases, Sally escorted her to the final security check. They parted with a kiss and it was a relief for both of them when Mary boarded the plane. It had not been an easy time for Sally.

Rumours circulated around the club and Sally had words with Helen. George was reported to be living in the east with a local woman but no one knew if that was true. Soji refused to believe anything bad about his friend.

Mary and Sally meet on the infrequent occasions Sally gets to England. They talk about the club, Wole and his family, and Nigeria, but never about George.

Crossing borders

"Tell them you're Canadian, tell them you're Canadian."

"I'm British and I have a valid visa in my passport which I have with me. Why should I lie? It'll only take a few minutes and we'll be on our way."

We are crossing the bridge from Niagara Falls, Ontario to Niagara Falls, New York; there are six people in the car, five Canadians and me. It is a very cold night and we are all very well-dressed.

"Where are you from?" asks the American border guard.

"Canada, Canada, Canada, Canada, Canada, the UK."

"May I see your passport, sir?"

The young officer clumsily thumbs through my passport, his gloves are a hindrance but I don't blame him for not removing them as this is a bitterly cold night.

"Pull under the canopy and follow me to the office."

My companions are telling me they told me so as I get out into the cold night air. Inside the office I get some pleasure as the officer thumbs through my well-used passport. He frowns and raises his eyebrows as he looks at one or two of the multi-coloured African visas. He seems to be nodding his head at every page and asks me where we are going. I tell him we are going to see a blues group fronted by Shaking Smith in a bar that takes Canadian dollars at par. That seems to amuse him and he staples a white card into my passport and explains that it's good for six months; it will ease my passage into the USA. There are smiles all around and they hope I'll have an enjoyable evening. The formalities having been completed, I am out into the cold night air and back in the car within a couple of minutes. I then attempt to answer the numerous questions of my young fellow passengers. They all regularly cross this border without hindrance and they only have to show their drivers licences.

The last time I was in Niagara Falls, New York it had looked run down but tonight, on closer inspection, it now looked like a bomb site. I thought Governor Cuomo should spend a few dollars in this desolate place as the comparison with the town across the river was unacceptable. The Canadian side is so clean and tidy, and also well lit. This city is the pits.

Shaking Smith is good but I prefer Canadian beer to the American stuff.

This winter's night was far removed from another memory of a border crossing in Africa. Everything was different but somehow the same and that vision came flooding back into my mind. Again, I was a passenger and the car was driven by a friend — a Nigerian. Instead of six in the car there had only been three of us: Wole my friend and driver, me in the front seat and in the back seat a young Ghanaian boy. This boy was a servant of a friend of ours; we had picked him up in Ikeja. He sat like a king in the back seat. He was a pleasant boy who spoke good English. We were speeding down the Badagary Road on our way from Lagos to the border with the Republic of Benin. It was good to be leaving the chaos of Lagos traffic and this was a good well-built road with little traffic. Wole was a road engineer and this day out was a sort of busman's holiday for him. Wole had spent many years in the UK and his wife was from Manchester. He worked for a tarmac company and this was a sort of inspection tour. He kept up a good commentary and at several sections he slowed down to inspect road repairs or freshly laid tarmac.

"I have to keep an eye on certain sections as sometimes the tarmac is thin as tar gets 'siphoned off'."

Wole and I had met in the Ikeja Country Club and our wives were good friends. Wole had told me about his inspection trip which would take him into Benin and asked if I would like to come along. The only snag was that I had to get a visa from the Benin Consulate in the centre of Lagos. I was all for seeing Benin.

I found the consulate in a depressingly dirty old building with an office that had seen better days. I was the only white man in the office which was crowded with people who seemed to be asleep in the heat. I was not sure if there was a queue so I made a beeline for a desk that had a clerk who seemed to be awake — big mistake, the clerk only seemed to speak Yoruba or basic French. He ushered me to another table that had several people standing around it. I thought I would have to wait my turn which was not to my liking in this hot and humid room. I was pleasantly surprised when the clerk rose, ignoring all the other people and motioned me to come forward. The clerk's English was good and he took my passport and money and asked me to have a seat. After about ten minutes I was wondering whether he was going to tell me to come back tomorrow, but much to my surprise he came out smiling and gave me my passport. I thanked him and woke some of the people who were sitting around his table.

When I told Wole about the visa process he laughed and said that I might have been the only white man asking for a visa that week. The clerk had obviously been waiting for someone to actually want a visa. I really didn't understand that last remark but I was to find out its truth later.

A few days later we set off and picked up the boy in the Government Residential Area GRA. The traffic along the Ikorodu Road into Lagos was very heavy but once we entered the Badagary Road it thinned out very fast. This road was, in part, quite near the sea and Wole explained that the sand base could shift and the road would sink. There were various spots that were continually under repair as the road had not been properly made. He was employed by the tarmac company and so they would have continuous work while the government could afford the expense.

Once out of Lagos the journey passed very quickly and we were fast approaching the border. This was a smooth ride and the sea on the left-hand side made it a very pleasant journey. Wole pointed out some fishing villages but that was not the only local occupation. This area was known for producing "brandy" and also for smuggling real spirits into Nigeria.

Just before we reached the border, Wole stopped the car and the boy got out. He then nonchalantly strolled across the border. Wole pulled up in front of the checkpoint where I got out and entered a place that was little more than a wooden shack. This place seemed to fit the wild surroundings with palms swaying in the fresh sea breeze and on the inland side of the road was a mangrove swamp. I was glad I had used mosquito spray as this was an ideal breeding ground. Inside the shack I was greeted by two very sleepy looking officials who took my passport and seemed to take an age to find the visa. As they stamped the visa one said, "What of driver?" I said that this was not my driver but my friend. I tried a bit of French but realised I had to call Wole into the shack. Wole came in smiling and gave one of the officials his card. They were all smiles and spoke very rapidly in Yoruba and with handshakes all round we were on our way.

Wole said they had told him this road was very good and they had not seen a white man for weeks.

As we drove off, we picked up the Ghanaian boy and I looked back to see if anyone was watching.

"Don't worry only white men get stopped at this border," Wole laughingly said.

We entered Cotonou, a small city, which was so different from Lagos. This city seemed so calm, clean and there were several white people walking around; I noticed a young white guy on a scooter driven by an African. This place seemed so friendly. Obviously, the pace of life was much slower than the hectic atmosphere of Lagos.

We had lunch in a restaurant where the owner was a French woman who seemed to know Wole. The food was excellent, quite tasty but not too spicy. I had a couple of glasses of good, rich, red wine with my lunch — this was heaven compared to Lagos. Wole had brought Sally here a few times and she had said they should live here, that it would be less expensive than Lagos. The problem was that all his family lived in Lagos and he had a house in Ikeja.

After lunch Wole suggested we buy some wine to take back to Lagos. I was all for it but Wole explained that we couldn't buy a bottle of wine without replacing the bottle with an empty. Luckily Wole had empty plastic containers in his boot — he was prepared. The wine was from grapes grown in Benin and this was the only wine I have ever had from that country. Wole said if we were stopped at the border, he would explain they were containers of engine oil. We bought our wine after

I demanded a free sample and we were on our way back to Lagos. Before we set off, we took a ride to the airport. It was very small and "guarded" by soldiers. Wole pointed out that all the soldiers we could see were asleep, so different from Lagos Airport.

There was no problem at the border, Wole just flashed his business card and they never even looked at my passport. It seems a pity that all border crossings are not so easy, even experienced travellers feel some tension in the hands of foreign border officials. There is also the tension of going from the known to the unknown, which takes its toll in sweat or increased blood pressure. In this case I was glad to return to Canada but loathe to leave sleepy Benin for aggressive Nigeria.

Stolen Car Radios

Easter Saturday, 1987, I wander down to the parking lot outside a hi-rise building in Guelph, Ontario. I have rented an apartment in the block for the summer and have been there just two days. Getting into my car I start the engine, buckle up and reach to start the radio. It is gone. I stare, I look away and then back again but it is not there! I can't believe it — this is not Lagos or Khartoum but Guelph Ontario. This is only the second time I have parked in this spot and Guelph is a quiet town: why my radio? I sit for a while in the stupid hope it will reappear, I even look under the seats.

As I drive, I start to think about Lagos: what a different place from Guelph, their only link was stolen radios. The biggest city in the largest black African nation in Africa and a medium-sized town in Canada, what could they have in common? Me, one or two Nigerian students and my radio linked them together. The radios were different, the mode of their missing was different, Lagos and Guelph are very different — they are in a different world and there is no comparison except a radio theft.

I had come to the conclusion that owning a car in every place is a liability. In Africa it can be a millstone and in Lagos a constant worry. Not long after arriving in Lagos I bought a new VW Passat (I later found out it had been made in South Africa, so much for the embargo.) A friend advised me not to buy a car with a radio, "That is the first thing they will pinch. If you want a radio buy a portable one with a cassette player and hide it under the seat."

That I did and my car was never broken into but my radio was stolen.

For a while I had a driver, considering Lagos an extremely difficult place to drive until I knew my way around. Later I decided to drive myself as my driver seemed to have lost his licence in mysterious circumstances, and he had to go back to his village to get a "new one". I found I preferred to drive myself and knowing plenty of short cuts I could avoid most of the traffic jams. Traffic in Lagos was, and almost certainly still is, chaotic, some might say anarchic (I prefer to think of anarchism as a political philosophy in no way related to the scary mess of Lagos traffic) particularly on the main roads. I learnt to navigate most of the back roads on Lagos mainland to avoid the traffic jams unless I was going to Lagos CBD, Victoria, or Ikoyi Islands. The back roads were poorly suited to vehicular traffic but were passable unless the rain was continuous. The sides of the roads had open sewers which were full even in dry weather. In the rainy season all manner of matter would wash across the roads; some of the garbage dumps near the sides of the road were as high as a two-storey building. The sights and smells were not bad enough to put me back into the heavy traffic, however.

The Lagos Government decided that to ease the traffic congestion, they would only allow certain vehicles into the city. If the vehicle first number was odd then they were allowed into the city on Mondays, Wednesdays and Fridays. Cars with even numbers were allowed in on Tuesdays, Thursdays and Saturdays. Sunday being a non-working day was unrestricted. My car had an even number so I could only go directly to work two days a week and the other days I had to go via the back roads. The back roads became very busy and there was a noticeable increase in vendors plying their wares from car to car. I had enough Yoruba to tell the vendors to get lost but driving to work in hot humid weather could be a trial of endurance. Luckily for me I worked on the edge of Lagos in an area called Yaba, at the University of Lagos. Yaba was where the car restrictions started on a flyover on the infamous Ikorodu Road.

One Monday morning I was on my way to work with a tape playing and fairly light traffic on the Ikorodu Road. I completely forgot the restrictions and as I reached the brow of the flyover the traffic jam started. I then noticed the odd numbers on the cars and realised I was in the wrong place. It's interesting that sweat produced by the heat and humidity became normal but an anxiety sweat is at once noticed. That happened to me as I saw a military policeman approaching my car. I had the presence of mind to switch off my tape deck and put it under the passenger seat.

He opened the passenger door and got in; there was nothing I could do he was the law. He was big and fat and I noticed he was a sergeant. Active duty would probably have killed him but my thoughts were maybe too unkind. I glanced at his uniform; it was a very faded green that may have not seen an iron for a while. Maybe his wife or wives had initially washed it in hard soap but were awaiting a present before ironing his uniform.

I told him I needed to go to the university but he told me I had to go to his barracks in Apapa. I pretended I didn't know the way but he obligingly told me he would show me the way. We left the main road and out of the traffic jam and I could tell that by using all the back streets it was going to take a long time to get to Apapa. We were talking in a form of West African Pidgin English, full of 'o's at the end of words, a stunted vocabulary and poor sentence construction. It was fun when used casually or in the UK but this was developing into a serious situation. He didn't come out with a direct demand for money (as I had hoped) but hinted at it by telling me how poorly paid they were in the army. He occasionally slipped into what I took to be Yoruba and I listened intently to see if I was being cursed. I tried to pick out words that would be about me or my "tribe".

It was warm but I was sweating more than normal and I noticed he was also sweating. I started to think that maybe I was giving him a harder time than he had expected. The last time two soldiers had jumped into my car in traffic I had sufficient money on me to satisfy them. That time they had said I had ignored their instructions to stop: "We say stop you no go 'gree' and you not stop." This time the red cap was being very evasive and I started to wonder whether he should have been on the Ikorodu Road. At one stage I thought I would stop the car, turn out my pockets to show him I had little money on me. That move might have angered him and I realised this was a situation where I was out of my depth. My Arab friends were good at dealing with these situations but this ordinary Brit felt inept, maybe impotent was a better word.

Suddenly his tone changed, he became friendlier and then he told me to stop the car. Now I was feeling very nervous. He got out of the car and told me I could go; I couldn't believe it and drove off before he could change his mind. As I drove, I was chuckling to myself, I couldn't believe my good fortune — there was no fathoming the African mind. Maybe he didn't want to go to the barracks, was he really even a soldier? All sorts of thoughts quickly passed through my mind and as I looked through the rear-view mirror, he was no longer visible. I turned a few corners and then decided I needed some music so I reached for the cassette player. It was gone. I stopped the car and searched under the seat but it was not there. My mind raced back to the Yaba flyover and I realised that the red cap, who had dominated a short piece of my life, had probably seen me hiding the player. How he had removed it without me seeing was a mystery, but I was concentrating on driving and listening to him.

I had been taken for a ride while I was playing mental games and not noticing a physical deception. Sometimes you win but in Lagos my "tribe" loses often. I decided to take the day off, and drove back home.

That was an expensive dash, I didn't make the same mistake again. Another learning experience in Lagos was the start of a conversation in Guelph.